HRH Prince Philip: Escape From The Palace

Thomas J O'Mara

Matador
9 Priory Business Park
Kibworth Beauchamp
Leicestershire LE8 0RX, UK
Tel: (+44) 116 279 2299
Fax: (+44) 116 279 2277
Email: books@troubador.co.uk
Web: www.troubador.co.uk/matador

ISBN 978-1783065-189

British Library Cataloguing in Publication Data.
A catalogue record for this book is available from the British Library.

Typeset in Aldine by Troubador Publishing Ltd
Printed and bound in the UK by TJ International, Padstow, Cornwall

Matador is an imprint of Troubador Publishing Ltd

To my dearly departed wife, Cecilia
and my three boys, Eoin, Niall and Conor.

No socks: no blasted socks

"Damn it to hell… bloody infernal thing."

I knock over a bottle of sauce as I gallop full pelt across the store. I'm in hot pursuit. As I look down at the red, gloopy mess on the floor; a tangled mass of glass and ketchup, Violet from Household and Haberdashery appears, all concern, arms flailing. What to do?

"Don't just look at it, woman! Never seen a broken bottle before? Where's the cleaner? Fetch the cleaner; quickly woman, before someone slips and does themselves an injury."

It's the usual busy Tuesday morning on the shop floor.

She scampers off and I stand guard, taking a moment to consider my life, for it seems to me altogether strange; so random, so utterly unbelievable. Here I am, His Royal Highness Prince Philip The Duke of Edinburgh, doing what I do best: apprehending thieves; the light-fingered. Shoplifters, to be precise. I am employed by the great F. W. Woolworth Company, that well-known and much-loved high street retailer. I'm in disguise, of course: a store detective. Nobody knows it's me, the Royal Consort, patrolling the aisles of Woolies, watching and waiting for the criminal-minded to pilfer from my esteemed paymaster. Complete accident you know, finding this job. One had certainly not planned for this form of employment: my alternative career, but fate had somehow plucked me from my safe, secure, royal bondage and deposited me in this busy London store, the Oxford Street branch. It all feels so bewildering, so… how should one put it...? mystifying. Why Woolies? Why West One? Could have been Marks and Spencer, Selfridges or even Harrods, one supposed, but no, here I am at nine forty-five a.m. on a delightfully sunny Tuesday morning doing what I do best: catching criminals; my new, exhilarating, clandestine occupation.

Hector Bellweather, the store manager, hears the kafuffle and descends the short stairs from his office, full of his manager grade three status. His office overlooks the shop floor. He doesn't miss much let me tell you, barely a thing from his elevated perch.

"What's this Mr Dukeof: another mishap?" he enquires.

"Dreadfully sorry sir," I reply. "In full flight you know, pursuing the culprit when somehow, I manage to veer slightly as I come around the corner and unfortunately dislodge a damned bottle of ketchup. Most dreadfully sorry, sir. Smaller bottle though, not large, thank heavens. Rather a mess though… sorry."

Hector is barely five foot five yet manages to look down on me with those withering eyes of his. He surveys the mess on the floor.

"There's a good chap," he says, "see it doesn't happen again. I may have to dock your pay."

"Yes sir, sorry sir; thank you… but I did catch the blighter. The police are on their way."

The day had started badly.

Socks. Where were the socks? There weren't any. No socks; no blasted socks. Can't get the staff, you know; at the palace, I mean. Soon got it sorted, though; resourceful: that's me; have to be; wore yesterday's! Bit whiffy of course, but needs must. Then the blessed key didn't work. Sticky you know, in the lock: damp most probably; jammed; wouldn't budge. Oil; needed oil. More delay, blast it; all I needed. Got away in the end; she who must be obeyed, still asleep. At least the bus was on time: the 74. Good route; excellent route. I got in at ten past eight. No sign of Clement; that's good, I thought: timekeeper; jobs worth! Gulped a cup of tea, slice of toast, straight to work. Checked my wig and spectacles; donned overcoat and tweed cap; pencil and notepad in pocket and off I went. Down the sweetie aisle first; my favourite, I have to say. Heaven and hell aisle I call it. Chocolate heaven and big arse hell, if you know what I mean. Ha, yes; best in town here at Woolies. Little wonder they can't resist… not that that's any excuse.

Didn't take long for the first.

There he was, bold as brass; just standing there gawping, helping himself. Short little bloke, plenty of girth, pocketing the 'pick and mix'. Didn't even pretend to fill a bag. Straight to the inside pocket. He thought he couldn't be seen. Well I saw him, the scoundrel; I bloody saw him. Way too early for an indulgence; silly boy; that's what I thought. Then up and

3

down Electrical he was; eye out for something small, maybe a plug. I saw him check me out. Too smart for the cadger. Made out I was choosing one of those new-fangled multi-headed screwdrivers. I'm not easy you know; got to be up early to catch me out. Could have jumped him there and then but one must wait, you see... be patient. Oh yes, patience. I'm used to that; waiting, waiting, waiting... yes, plenty of that in the other job: the royal handshaking job. Has to be leaving the store without paying; that's the thing; can't catch the rogue till one foot is out the door, pockets full. Then he's yours if you're quick enough and I always am; best either side of the Thames; make no mistake. Thieving rascals, all of them, coming in to dip their fingers. Women are the worst with their big bags and babies. I nabbed the rascal at the door and deposited him in the back office until the police came along. Same procedure every time here at Woolies; wait, watch, apprehend, arrest.

It had been a typical start to a typical day.

One can't always know at first: that's what I find. The strangest people shoplift. Not always the needy or the stupid, you know. Granted that bloke with the sweet tooth was, how should one put it, slightly dim; an egg or two short of a soufflé. But as long I've been doing this job, I've not been quite able to put my finger on it. I've had a judge and several nuns, traffic wardens of course, one or two so-called personalities and lots of kids loaded with dosh who did it for fun: spoiled; quite a few from the local grammar round the corner. Posh upstarts. Never can tell till you see them do it but I've got a keen eye even with the dark glasses. Love it, love it, I tell you; must be the breeding. Same as the navy really.

Old Monty would know. Like a mission, a covert mission: search and destroy; in my case search and arrest. It's a drug to me: a high as one of those hippy chaps might say. Have to do it. Keeps them honest the ones who know; keeps me sane the ones who don't, the ones I catch.

Bloody good at this but sometimes I knock over a blasted bottle of ketchup in the heat of battle. Then I have to pander to bloody grade three, jumped-up bloody Hector. Damn near takes all the good out of it… yes, damn near all of it… but not quite and I constantly have to remind myself the principal reason I do this job. Yes it's true, I love the thrill of the chase, the subterfuge, the sense of achievement when I deposit another ne'er-do-well into the hands of the law, but it would be entirely wrong of me to indulge simply for my own personal satisfaction; entirely wrong. One cannot place oneself ahead of one's duty. No no; there are far greater issues at stake than one's own personal concerns. I shall therefore, remain committed to apprehending as many low-life, shoplifting crooks as I can and shall pander to that vain, self-satisfied Mr Hector Bellweather, for however long my overall objective takes.

Elizabeth deserves nothing less.

A Freud case most definitely: not the painter

Prince Philip addresses the young lady therapist in front of him. He shakes her hand and she sits down.

"Nice to see you again," he says. "Excellent morning; shall we start? I know how this works. I get to speak, you get to listen; isn't that correct? Allow me to pour the tea."

The therapist takes out a laptop and a notepad. She nods in his direction.

The prince begins to move around the room, hands behind his back, muttering to himself as if not sure where to begin. Finally he stands by the window and stares out towards the park: Green Park, on the north side of the palace. He raises a questioning finger and addresses the young professional.

"So you know your history, eh? Got a good memory,

young lady? Can you tell me what happened in nineteen sixty-six? Yes, a long time ago; well before your time, I'd imagine. You might not have even been born. The swinging sixties and all that. Remember? Well let me tell you, I do. I remember like it was yesterday.

"Spring, sixty-six. I was forty… forty-five back then. Not quite as fit as the fabled flea, but working out, you know; exercise, horses, that sort of thing... cricket; young family; busy, busy, busy: dinners, functions, receptions. Open this, sample that: smash the magnum; fully functioning you know; up to speed; a paid-up member of the family, 'The Firm' as we're called; well grounded. Knew my stuff and just as important, knew my place. That's the key to the royals, you know; a place for every royal and for every royal their place!"

He takes a long slow sip from his tea and turns to his interviewer. His eyes narrow.

"My job you ask, way back then… support mostly: Her Majesty in her official duties; follow the leader, there's a good boy, keep up. Offer a well-appointed observation here and there. That was my favourite part; indulging in my famous witty repartee. What else? The weather of course; will it rain? The good cause, the excellent work, the undoubted loveliness of it all, the dedication. Love to come again, madam chairperson; absolutely."

He checks the young lady has no questions and carries on.

"The press: loved it; easy copy, you see: the royals this, the royals that… the public too, still do, of course: part of the system; doing one's bit for the country, you understand. And not just for The Queen. Had my own duties, in addition. Now let me think, nineteen sixty-six… there was the World

Wildlife, the Award scheme, industry, Commonwealth, chairing this and that charity. Then there were my hobbies, for want of a better description. Yes, oh yes, the flying, the research, books and speeches, all manner of horsey activity: Have I mentioned that before? Sometimes one repeats oneself. Lots more besides, what else...? Children; mustn't forget one's children; four of them, youngest coming up to two... rascals. Hadn't a moment to myself. Busy, as I've said; rushed off my feet.

"Here's the thing. I was miserable: full of it, I was: full of a silly inexplicable melancholy. I can see that look in your eye. Can't quite believe it, can you? Well neither could I, let me tell you. I had it all: all of it, you see... the status, the respect, the family. So important, you know, one's family... couldn't have asked for more. Heaven knows I was privileged; still am, undoubtedly; a Freud case most definitely... not the painter. Auntie would have known and mother. Everything and nothing. That was it, everything and bloody nothing. Who said it? Some noisy pop band or other, I believe: shades of grey... no black, no white: only bloody, infernal grey. The swinging sixties: kaleidoscope of colour everywhere and I'm the only depressed man in the world. Sometimes it got really bad. I went right into myself, my own little self-absorbed world; weeks on end; monumentally sorry for myself; trying to keep a sense of perspective, balance. Trying, so hard, so very, very hard; trying, trying... failing."

The prince becomes irritated as he relives the bad times and turns to his therapist.

"Why am I bleating like this? Already said too much. Wasn't raised to bleat, you know. Won't get out, will it? Will it...? Don't care. Have to tell someone and you're, well... here to listen; well paid I trust, aren't you? No disrespect intended. But you're so young... we all have to earn a crust. I understand. Therapy. Is that what you call it? One must do certain things to maintain the balance, the equilibrium of one's life, one's mental state, as you know. And this is mine, my therapy; telling you... so they inform me. God alone knows why. You're a stranger, an independent observer. No prejudices... I hope. You do like the royals? One supposes you must...

"In any case, I'm not that bothered. Listen if you want. Write your bloody notes, if that's what you want. It's all ancient history you see, but you might be just a tad surprised or even interested. The monarchy would have been so different, so very different were it not for a series of extraordinary events coming together, and this story, the one I'm about to tell, isn't one you will find in any history book. Why? Because it never happened. He who wins the war writes the history. Old Winston said that. I liked old Winston. Smart! He won and I won, you see... won the war: so we both wrote the bloody history: and, my little secret; well it never happened; that's why; none of it, a history *not* written has never happened. The world will never know what I'm about to tell you."

He looks out across The Queen Victoria monument and down the red tarmacked Mall.

"Looking back, I'm still not sure what to make of it all. What was I? Wise, wilful, rash, ridiculous? Was I blessed with the innocence of a brave knight on a noble quest or was I driven by the desperate despair of a man with nothing left to lose...? Was I mad? I have no answer but I shall tell you one thing, young lady, it was bloody astounding, nothing less, and I'm the better man for it and the monarchy, the stronger for it… mark my words!

"As I said, listen if you're bothered; write if you want. No skin off my nose. No bloody difference to me."

He looks over to the therapist. Head down, she has already written several pages of shorthand and her tea has gone cold.

She carries no money, I carry no worth

Every night I lie on my bed and stare at the ceiling, my life and circumstance perform before me. My words and thoughts replay.

I am tall, blond, bright and able.

I am powerful, insightful and proud. Decisive and astute, success knows my name. I love and am loved. I have it all. People look at me and bow and defer. They listen, curious, when I speak. My cup overflows.

Palace on The Mall. Strident, inspiring, built by and for the Empire. Imperious and majestic; shamelessly flaunting its importance at every subject and every passing stranger. I live here in this palace full of pomp, full of ceremony: befitting the splendour of a royal family: my family.

I have nothing.

I have lost everything; my pride, my purpose, my soul. I

walk the stuttering, shuffling meander of a mediocre second best; always one step adrift, one step behind; soulless. An excuse for a human being, I have shamefully taken The Queen's shilling. She carries no money. I carry no worth. This waste of space is what I have become: meaningless: surplus to my own requirement.

Save me.

Someone, somehow, somewhere. For pity's sake rescue me from a thousand insincere greetings, ten thousand hollow handshakes.

Polite applause. Wonderful occasion. Joint royal waves. How do you do? Thank you. Yes indeed, very impressive. Too kind, much too kind. Allow me, Ma'am. Hold your empty purse while you cut the ribbon, pop the cork, smash the bottle. Clip and snip and glide inside.

Enough, enough. Fool! Pull yourself together man. Stand up straight. Do your duty you lily-livered buffoon. You're a prince of the realm. Have you no pride, no self-respect? Remember! Remember! Lonely child, abandoned child: that's what I was; an itinerant teen with no home to call my own but did I buckle, succumb? Not me! Never. Cold showers, cold food, cold bed, but a hot fiery Germanic temper, burning with desire; never-say-die. The will to overcome, to succeed, is all mine. For heaven's sake, you're a survivor; unique; nobody can take that away. This is nothing, nothing at all. Front up man, for pity's sake. Won't last forever. How can it? Chest out, chin up, purposeful stride; just like a royal.

What's that song... on the wireless? Where is that wireless? Quiet please, for a moment. Oh wait... ah yes. I like this one. I do like this one, this melody.

Flies the bird through the air
Swims the fish through the sea
For I'll never be bound
For I'll always be free

Yes indeed, time to stare again at the dark shadows on the ceiling and on the walls and to wait and wait till a new day dawns.

My belly grumbles.

Seven-thirty already. Starved. Need breakfast; egg and toasted soldiers. Never whine on an empty stomach; that's my motto.

The Germans, not the blasted Germans again

The Queen is annoyed, frustrated. She addresses her tardy husband with a barely concealed fury.

"Philip please; do hurry. You're the last down to breakfast… again. One should never be late but I fear this is becoming an intolerable habit."

Her Lady-in-Waiting hands her a scarf and matching gloves and Her Majesty hovers close to the door. Her face is scrunched up; tight and furrowed and full of dissatisfaction. There's just a tinge of hurt in her eyes. She is 'Her Majesty', after all. One should not have to ask for the minimum deference one is entitled to. Acquiescence should be forthcoming, given freely by her subjects in public and by her family in private. Goodness, it's so obvious. And Philip, her husband of all people; he should know. This is ridiculous. One is upset; one is very upset.

A controlled intake of breath is followed by a sigh of unrequited annoyance. She shuffles vaguely from foot to foot while her husband, carefully avoiding eye contact, peers over his unappetising breakfast and busies himself with the lukewarm offerings. His soldiers are soft and bendy, his tea, tepid with a scum forming around the edges. His scrambled eggs are in a sorry state; congealed and squelchy; they look up from the plate, as if daring the prince to eat. He almost does but, in the end thinks the better of it. His eyes fall on his daily newspaper, *The Telegraph*, lying unopened beside the toast, but feeling a regal fury hovering near the door, he decides against it and instead double-gulps his tea and mangles and chews his defeated soldiers.

In the far corner, which has been newly modernised and shelved, young Prince Charles has turned on the radio so that he and Anne can catch the latest pop music from Radio Caroline before they are whisked off to their respective schools. He keeps the volume down so as not to attract The Queen's attention… but fails.

"Charles, please; turn that infernal noise off," The Queen groans. Her eyes roll, her lips quiver.

"But Mother, I shall keep it low, very low… just until Jones comes. This one is really good. It's by a new group Mother. Listen."

Gentle guitar sounds waft into the room and both Charles and Anne hum along. The dogs have run over to the corner and look curiously at the strange noisy box before losing interest, preferring instead to return and beg at Prince Philip's feet.

"Is there any more tea? And this egg: it's cold and… "

"No Philip, it's your own fault. We have so much to do: organise the day, check the summer schedule, review the guest list, not to mention get oneself ready. You do know the Germans are invited?"

Philip shrugs, winces and tears a grudging mouthful.

Near the window, one of the male corgis jumps up on the highest seat, but his reign is cut short by the dominant female and he's rapidly dispatched, whining and yelping back to the pack. He paws at the window, looking for a way out.

"The Germans? Not the blasted Germans again; too much of a good thing."

He hears the music and turns his head, his mood suddenly improving.

"Good heavens Charles. That song, I know it; I know that one. I've heard it before; lovely… soothing… ah yes, do turn it up."

and I'll find my way home
yes I will, yes I will
through the rain and the snow
and the cold winter chill

The Queen's frown deepens. Her eyes narrow, her back stiffens.

"No you shall not, Charles. I shan't tell you again. Turn that abject gadget off. Find your satchel. You too Anne; comb your hair. Philip, the car is here. We have to leave now."

The valet arrives with coats and the family jump in the waiting transport. Husband and wife eye each other.

The Queen softens.

"I'm sorry Philip. I know one's sleep is difficult at present, but you really must make a greater effort."

"I agree absolutely; no excuses Elizabeth. I simply must improve. What a dreadful example I have become."

"We'll speak later darling Philip; not now, not in front of the children; perhaps after dinner. I also have something on my mind; something strange that happened on Saturday and your opinion would be greatly appreciated."

"Ou est les pommes de terre?"

"It's probably nothing, Philip; you know how I worry."

The Queen is pacing, wringing her hands, mouthing silent words. She picks up a napkin and looks into the distance towards Australia Gate and the West Island, but sees nothing of the London skyline or the gathering clouds on a darkening, misty night. Overlooking the parade ground, this is her favourite room; comfortable, quite ordinary really, with its deep, warm couches, well-worn tables and chairs and the newly installed two-bar electric heater she finds so practical. Her Majesty can relax here, take stock and recount the day's concerns. Her husband sits and listens.

"I'm concerned about Charles, Philip. One hesitates to say, but he seems to have a rather cavalier attitude towards responsibility, towards work. Have you noticed? Have you seen his results from Gordonstoun?"

She carries on, neither awaiting nor requiring a reply.

The prince nods and Her Majesty continues, unaware she is strangling the blameless napkin.

"On Saturday, if you remember, I sent him to dig out some potatoes for Sunday's dinner, as you and I had agreed, and of course he said yes; keen to help apparently. But later, perhaps after an hour or so, when he was playing cricket with the head-gardener's son, I enquired. I called him over, mid-innings, and referred to the fact that no potatoes were forthcoming. There was, I pointed out, a bucket, regrettably short of potato. 'Ou est les pommes de terre?' I said – you know he's doing French this year."

"Ou *sont* les pommes de terres," the prince interrupts, thoughtfully. "The plural, dear: 'sont'."

Her Majesty ignores her husband's comment and continues.

"He was, thankfully, suitably embarrassed, and I believe blushed a little. He said he was about to dig them out but that he had had to wait… 'had to wait', Philip! What on earth did he mean? I was so taken aback I simply dared not ask. But strangely, he then proceeded back down the garden in his wellingtons with fork and gloves and bucket: that new plastic one."

One corner of Her Majesty's napkin, by now under severe pressure, defers to her will, stretching and straining, deforming visibly by the second, distended within a thread of its very existence yet hanging on fiercely as only a royal napkin can.

The Queen again looks out the window, retracing Charles's steps in her mind's eye.

The room becomes silent except for the tick-tock of the

19

nearside wall clock and a slight twanging sound from the far side of the room, near The Queen Mother's chair.

"Do you think he has, how should one put it, a weakness Philip? One's family have been known to, on occasion… be slightly erratic… and yours of course; even more so."

Philip considers.

"Perhaps he has a lot on his mind; teenagers can be forgetful, you know. Gordonstoun again next week; I'm not sure he's all that settled. Might be anxious or a tad forgetful. So what did you do dear?"

The Queen sits down in her large, red recliner, and carefully examines the distended napkin, swapping her attention to one of the lesser-molested corners.

"Naturally, one does not wish to exaggerate or indeed exacerbate. I did nothing. I decided not to pursue the issue. Filled a full bucket in the end but there was no proper explanation forthcoming. He simply said they were ready when he went the second time. They were 'ready', Philip! Of course they were ready! Potatoes are always ready! What on earth did he mean? One is perplexed, darling, very much so."

She sighs and fidgets.

"Perhaps I worry too much."

The Prince takes out his pipe, his favourite, the Seafarer's Friend; made from the hardest teak. He examines both ends before whacking it briskly against the side of his chair, sending charred remains flying in all directions. A passing corgi briefly samples the discarded contents, recoils, and trots away.

"Oh it's nothing to worry about Liz, teenager stuff… perhaps a girl."

"And what do you think, Mother?"

At the far side of the room The Queen Mother has suddenly burst into life as she tries to swat an annoying fly, a bluebottle. She has always had an aversion to flies of every description but especially the slim dark American invader who disturbs the native and upsets the natural order of things – nineteen thirty-six was a particularly bad year. This particular insect is much too quick for her and seems to regard the swish and swoop of her big plastic swatter as a gentle work-out.

"I beg your pardon, Elizabeth," she says, "this horrid creature… "

Again she flails at an empty space where one's fly should be.

"What appears to be the matter, Elizabeth?"

"It's Charles, Mother. Have you noticed anything… peculiar?"

The Queen Mother pulls her chair, the floral upholstered, to the centre of the room, climbs up on it and peers at the ceiling rose. She conducts an unseen orchestra with her plastic baton, waving it frantically left and right, wasting no effort in her attempts to swat the annoying intruder.

"Charles?" she says, never taking her eye off the target. "No, not a jot; same delightful, considerate boy he has always been… now where has that pesky little…?"

She leans forward against the back of the chair, swishing with vigour this way and that, her chair not knowing what to do. Her spare arm extends, ballet-like, out behind and she wobbles dangerously, like a tightrope walker rocked by a sudden gust of wind. Philip nods and the butler moves slowly forward, arms nervously extended, hoping his reputation as a safe fifteen under the Garryowen will not be tested.

"Mother, please. Come down from there. One could do oneself an injury."

The Queen Mother comes down and The Queen breathes a sigh of relief. Again she paces but relaxes a little.

"Well perhaps I am a little over-anxious."

She pours a small scotch from the cabinet and hands it to her husband. She pours a large one for herself and a larger for her mother. She sits down and takes several sips before becoming restless again. She glances over at her husband.

"And what of you Philip? Have you applied yourself to 'the issue'?"

A plume of blue-grey smoke fills the air and Philip stares into the far beyond.

"I have Elizabeth," he replies. "It's not an issue at all, no-no, not at all. We are royals are we not? Each with one's place and duty. One must discharge one's obligations. I fully intend to discharge mine."

The Queen smiles.

"Let that be an end to it then. No more bad tempers Philip; no more foul moods. You are so much more handsome with a pleasant face; one's dependable liege man; one's immovable rock."

The prince remains silent, deep in thought and smoking his pipe, whilst the blue-grey cloud deepens and blackens, hanging directly above his head.

German blood, Greek heart, British spirit

God plays with me just for the hell of it.

You see on the following day, I remember it well, I woke up, still full of the melancholy. Prince Consort I may have been, father to the future King of England; supposedly a man of substance, of some importance, but I was trapped: totally completely and utterly.

I felt like a prize idiot, a fish out of water, every inch a Johnny Foreigner in some far-flung land; the man who had made the most monumental mistake and who had, unbelievably, taken fifteen years to find out. I looked out the window to see. They were large again today, huge: more so than yesterday, and much more so than the day before: cliff-faced slabs of rock: craggy, belligerent, black as coal. What the hell are you doing? Answer me! Why...? as if rocks could answer! Her Majesty's words of last evening scorned in in my ears. 'No more bad tempers,' she had said, 'so much more handsome with a pleasant face.' What did she think I was; some sort of performing monkey? I'm a liege man... a liege *man*, not a liege *puppet*.

It wasn't always like this, you know. In the early days there weren't any; mountains I mean. The harbour of my mind's eye was clearly visible: look south; out across Victoria Station and down to the mighty Thames. The river: calm, the frigate: shipshape, moored tight against anything and everything an enemy could muster. Crisp uniform, fresh blue sky; greet the day. The MG down through Buckingham Gate; dash along. Assume command; happy crew, happier commander; God in his heaven.

Perhaps after the second tour, or was it after Charles's or Anne's arrival or perhaps both; one finds it so difficult to remember the exact sequence of events. In any case, early on in the marriage, the hills began to emerge. Just there: bleak hills, not mountains, every morning; outside my window looking in at me, goading. The control-bridge was still visible over the crest for a time, but deck and guns eventually became obscured, sunk beneath the skyline: no real problem I thought, before it became serious: a creeping gradual onslaught. No need to panic; maintain control; plot a steady course and navigate safe passage; an even keel. It will pass, whatever this damned thing is. Stiff upper lip and all that; more vital now than ever.

"What are you staring at Philip?"

Too often The Queen caught me unawares and I would stumble back to reality.

"Nothing dear. Just the weather. Old mariner habits: the weather; first thing every morning; what will it do, darling... Will it rain?"

I'm not a vain man in the conventional sense. Yes, when asked, one may admit to, as a young man, a degree of ambition, ability, desire. But even I was surprised. First grey hair arrived, unacknowledged of course, until at least a hundred more of the invading blighters displayed themselves; the gradual thinning; the uninvited paunch despite fifty tough ones; Bullworker you know, every morning before breakfast... if there was time. Looked in the mirror; freckles became blotches; tufts of hairs where they didn't belong, not enough where they did; chunks of Savannah bushland over each eye. Ha, yes, perhaps I was vain after all. But so much worse than all that was the early morning wretchedness. It was becoming more and more difficult to conquer the blasted inertia of my daily life and those feckless hills were becoming larger and larger; more than hills: mountains. By the time I was combing as much salt as pepper, I rarely looked for the harbour. I knew it was there: same place, same distance, out across Victoria Station, but the obstacles had morphed as if some kind of blasted spaceship from Mars had descended and hauled and yanked and heaved the very earth between me and my harbour and turned the whole ungodly thing into some impassable range of Himalayas. I became, you know, hate to say it... depressed. Didn't know what to do; frightened: a cowering fox facing a howling pack. I even considered a quack remedy; man enough to admit.

"I want some pills."

The doc looked at me, eager to please. I had the choice.

25

He held up the bottles. The lemon in the morning followed by the strawberry, twice-a-day, or the stronger blackcurrant before bed. Fruit pills! I worried, felt shameful, and in the end I said no. I'm a royal you know, a royal. German blood, Greek heart, British spirit. I can overcome this on my own, I said, and not a word to you know who. It's just a check-up.

I determined to face them down. I knew those blasted mountains would be there each and every morning but I looked the blackness dead in the eye and said no; the prince was not for turning! Sometime later a variation of that little phrase became quite popular with a certain Mrs Thatcher.

Tough, you ask, this damned depression?

Let me tell you… impossible. Wretched things, the mountains, threatened to invade the bedroom: pressed against the window panes. I could feel them almost before I woke up. I lay there, not wanting to open my eyes. Can't have been good for the family, what with our dicky emotions. We're all temperamental, we royals, sometimes bordering on nastiness; tempers shorter than a gnat's elbow. But the public never knew. No, no. Always smile for the adoring public and wave; don't forget to wave. Would have been a scandal. I can see it now, scoop after scoop. Prince Philip this, Duke of Edinburgh that; break-down, scandal, crisis. So tough for all of us and me with my short little fuse; a schooner tossed about, mercilessly, on the high sea.

We all bore up.

Liz was a trouper and the children; proud of them. The Queen Mother; plenty on her plate too; widowed too young, you know. And Margaret, with the endless kafuffle over her private life. Not sure how much each of them knew. Not much, I expect. Elizabeth shielded them from the worst, and rightly so. Of course, The Queen Mother was, by then, far more interested in our four-legged friends: Aintree, Ascot, that sort of thing. As for myself, fortunately there were the endless distractions. Cut this ribbon; open that door; shake the waiting hand. Wonderful smell of paint and plenty to eat, as long as you enjoyed cucumber sandwiches. Played games with myself; guess the colour from the smell – the paint not the sandwiches. Then we'd step inside. Do hope all this paint is made in Britain. Travel, travel, travel: walking, cycling, cars, carriages, planes, yachts and rail... even the tube. Aren't the royals ever-so good to take the tube? Like we're human or something! Some of those hacks were good, mind; worried a bit. Sniff-out a story soon as you'd say 'How-do', but no, not even the daily pen-pushing sniffer dogs from Fleet Street could breach the royal barriers and the staff: one hundred per cent loyal. My preoccupation remained '*my*' preoccupation: the black hills of Buckingham Palace were '*my*' black hills... private!

Funny thing about mountains. They're fascinating, don't you think? No two the same. I became something of an expert. Read everything and watched all those nature programmes. Those brave souls, Hilary, Tensing, for example, climbed and conquered whilst others climbed and failed. Brave men, all of them, facing those blasted mountains. Now it was my turn; my time. I can and I will, I decided; have to. Chin up man; time to tackle my own mounting demons.

Then something truly amazing happened. I didn't expect it. No; certainly didn't see it coming but one, as The Queen Mother used to say, must never look a proverbial gift horse in its proverbial mouth. I grabbed it with both hands... not the horse, you understand.

It was shortly after one of those elaborate but excruciatingly boring dinners at the palace. Had to be done of course, for Britain and for the Commonwealth. Elizabeth constantly reminded me, lest I forgot; the French I think, or the Spanish. I took the midnight air as I was wont to do, in the west-facing garden. Warm night, I remember. The potatoes had been dug out and the lettuce by the south wall, Charles's patch, was being nibbled again. The gardener wanted to set traps but I said no. Conservation begins at home. Birds prey on slugs, you know. Furry things have to eat. Wouldn't do for me to preach conservation to the Africans but wallop some enterprising rabbit on one's own vegetable patch, now would it? Won't starve for the want of feeding of a few furry creatures, I said.

It was when I stepped inside again, and undertook the walk of shame beneath the portraits of those more-worthy-than-I predecessors, that I noticed Jones, our head butler, polishing the silver. Polishing I thought, at this hour? Spoons I think, or perhaps the silver napkin rings; it mattered not, of course, it was the hour: one o'clock. What was he doing, polishing at that hour of the morning? When I went over, I realised he looked at least as troubled as I and not at all keen to engage in conversation.

"Can't sleep then?" I ventured, intending to put him at his ease. I always have time for staff prepared to place themselves above and beyond the call of duty, even if uncalled-for, at some unholy hour of the night.

"Beg your pardon sir," he replied. "It's not my place and

I was unsure, and wondered sir, if perhaps you could offer a suggestion."

"Beg your pardon what," I replied "What the devil are you talking about. Are you short of help, an assistant? It's gone one o'clock, for heaven's sake. You should be in bed."

"Well," he continued, "I was aware of your garden walks and wanted a quiet word, beg your pardon, sir. I don't know what to do… it's a little delicate."

I like to think I'm a fair man, especially in areas of staffing and staff welfare but I was, despite my best efforts, starting to become a little irritated. We have perfectly legitimate and clearly-defined staff procedures in situ, at all palaces and castles for precisely such matters. Wrote them myself, so I know they're good! Had more than enough on my plate without this introverted buffoon accosting me in the middle of the night, with some petty grievance.

I fixed him with a stare.

"Out with it man."

"There's a hole sir, which doesn't belong to anybody."

"A hole?"

"Yes sir. I've checked the handbook. Not me, as far as I can tell, nor the valet sir, nor the footman or equerry and I can't see why any of the domestics or clerks in the back office would want it."

Stood there and thought; how absurd: two demented nuts discussing a homeless hole at one in the morning.

"Well you'd better show me then."

You conniving, jumped-up old tart. What are you hiding from me?

I serve two old ladies!

Well, it's a bit naughty of me, a Royal Consort describing my darling wife Elizabeth in such terms, but Buckingham Palace; no reservations, none at all; beautiful building and extremely interesting, but a secretive old lady nonetheless.

I love old Buck Palace. Hefty dollop of bricks and mortar, don't you think? She speaks to me, commands me, bosses me about. I do her bidding, happy to! Alcoves, attics, basements, bedrooms, balustrades, reception rooms, grand halls, pictures and portraits, crevices, cornices, chandeliers, statues, stairs and steps, all the bits and bobs here and there. My predecessors were busy bees indeed and left behind a marvellous legacy. I am the royal-incumbent premier, bar Elizabeth, of course, and I look after the majestic old pile – the palace I mean – have done since the early fifties. I thought I knew everything about her, the lot; no secrets.

She was in a bit of a state when Elizabeth and I first took over just after the war when we got married: adversity, you know; every penny counts, not like today! Needed major upgrading: couldn't allow the royal showpiece to remain in such a shabby state, could we? Money had to be found from somewhere and lots of it. The prime minister, Mr Churchill; very supportive… in the end.

"Winston, we need money."

"I'm terribly sorry, Your Royal Highness; impossible; constraints, shortages, you know; the country's flat broke."

"Well, could we rent out a wing or two, earn a little extra?"

"Buckingham Palace! Rent! Absolutely not."

"No, no Winston, not the touristy bits or the art rooms. No, rather, I was thinking, maybe round the back, down the far end, away from it all; knock a hole in the west wall; their own entrance; let me see: conversions; one and two-bed apartments; a mews, gallery or two… prime location you know! And off-street parking; no difficulty renting. I've even got the name, 'The Winston Churchill Parade'. What do you say? Elizabeth won't mind; we'll still have plenty of room… Are you feeling all right Winston?"

"Stop! Stop! You've made your point sir." Winston's face had turned red. "How much do you need?"

Just what the doctor ordered you know, now that my navy career was over. New to the job and a new job to do: fabulous project, back in fifty-three. Rolled-up my sleeves and got on with it. Years of toil and a mountain of cash, that's what it required; no two ways. Public so very generous… and Winston, of course, with a little persuasion! Spend, spend, spend. Major success, though. Did country and Commonwealth proud: our Buckingham Palace: royal splendour restored.

Thought I knew our stately abode inside and out, but did I?

I followed old Jones down the dimly-lit rooms and corridors at one-thirty in the morning: The State Rooms. Those ancient wigged and crusty-faced royals cast a judgemental eye on me from their lofted perches, but I felt alive: a sense of purpose. We had an understanding, you see, old Buck House and I. We understood each other; practically married to the place in the end. No secrets from her, or so I thought. She also knew a lot about me. These palace walls had witnessed my early-morning despair, listened uncomplaining to my grumps and groans, the floors creaking in sympathy with my heavy footsteps; at least I hope it was sympathy! Those same lofty ceilings oversaw my restraint, my determination, my will to overcome. Oh yes, damned right, this place knew me, knew my very soul. But as I stepped along with Jones I began to think I may be mistaken.

You conniving, jumped up old tart. What are you hiding from me? Are you hiding something? I wondered.

I scowled at Jones. "Good grief man, this had better be good."

He led me along. "This way, sir."

He was muttering to himself under his breath; not his fault; what was he to do, that sort of thing. Duty to report, he mumbled, but to whom? And he glanced accusingly at me.

Instructions: no good, who to ask. He was hunched over, feet shuffling, white gloves jolting as he strode along. His linen polishing cloth was slung over his shoulder as we made our way to the family rooms.

"Should be in bed," he muttered.

"Well so should I," I retorted. "Nincompoop."

That shut him up.

Very difficult I find, to maintain one's sense of calm whilst on some whacky, bleary-eyed, goose chase! Checked I was following him several times as we upped stair and crossed corridor, his sombre greying head bobbing up and down as we went. We arrived at my bathroom, of all places, where he knocked and pushed the door at the same time, as if not quite sure what the protocol was for the circumstances.

"In you go, sir; over there," and he switched on the light. I looked around.

It's a good size, my bathroom. Usual fare: toilet, bath, shower; all done out in Edinburgh green. Nothing unusual I thought, and then, perhaps a little too quickly, I felt my temper flare in his direction.

"Now look here, Jones. I've had quite enough of this… silliness. It's late. We're both up early in the morning so why don't we both just call it a night and…"

Oblivious to me and the world, he ducked under the sink beside the cistern.

"I really must insist," I continued. "Come out from there."

But before I had finished, he twisted some sort of lever and a two-foot square panel grinded to his left and behind the toilet. The panel was more than a little stiff, I noticed; needed oiling.

"The plumber reported to me, sir, yesterday morning, after the leak… but to whom do I report? Nothing in the instructions, sir. I thought the section on 'Maintenance and Repair' or 'Emergency Procedure – Reporting Protocol' might help, but… "

I went over and looked into it. Naturally, I saw nothing. It was a black hole after all but I was instantly intrigued.

"Heavens above; wonder where it leads," I thought out loud.

Jones was stood beside the door, yawning.

"Who else knows about this?" I questioned.

"Nobody sir: you see the instruction manual was rather vague as to how one should proceed, so… "

I cut him off. "And the plumber?"

Jones raised his index finger. "Told him it could be a national security issue, not to say a word, and that I would take upon myself to make the appropriate enquiries."

"That's excellent," I said. "Well done. Not a word to a soul. Is that understood? Come to my bedroom for ten p.m. tomorrow night… and bring along a torch."

8

Sometimes God plays nice

As a child, I always loved adventure; a raft to build, a cave to investigate, a frog or two to hide in the laundry basket. I was a cheeky boy: a lad, one might say these days. Never lost it, never! The excitement of some new exploration or challenge, or the fun of seeing a sister leap six foot in the air. Hoots of laughter, generally followed by a whack on the ear… my ear. And now, not the same. How could it be? Have to behave; yes sir, yes sir, three bags bloody full sir. No, not the same, nor should one expect it to be, of course. But no sense of humour these so-called courtiers. All so bloody stiff, the lot of them.

Well, there I go again, another little whinge. Made my bed, I suppose…

Now my practical jokes have to be ever-so… *not* funny. Hardly worthwhile, really. Most fun I get these days is teasing the secretary pool with some shorthand nonsense in French gobbledygook and seeing what they come up with or sending a young stable hand for the camouflaged pony in the far stable. Immensely funny, I think you'll agree, but you know, despite my undoubted sense of humour, most people appear to be quite scared of me. Amazing don't you think? But there you have it; scared stiff. Can't think why. They just smile meekly and hope I go away; can see it in their eyes. Sad really.

Baiting the press... that's my favourite. Say something oblique, something that can be taken in more ways than one, and let them try to squeeze something sensible out of it for the next morning's paper. I was once served frankfurters by a rather plump German lady and I commended her, loudly, on her delightful sausages. Well rounded, I said, and asked her if she enjoyed one or two herself. Well, she was rather plump. Burst out laughing, to ease the resulting tension. Oh the fun of it; harmless of course; the perplexed faces of the hacks trying to paraphrase was wonderful. That's as far as one can go, these days. The Queen worries, you know.

"Philip! Does one wish to cause another diplomatic incident?"

Back in sixty-six, I recall, I had more pressing worries.

Those blasted mountains, first thing every morning. I knew what they were: retribution, that's what; punishment for my weakness. To the world, I was the most privileged man alive but to those mountains, shoving their way through my window, I was the target; the quarry. Out to get me, the blighters; out to crush my heart and soul and spirit and whatever small part of me remained unsullied. But I would not allow them. Something always came along to lessen the burden; new babies, four of them in fact, a pot of cash from the government to tart the old place up, and when I got really, really lucky, a hidden tunnel; my very own secret, forbidden tunnel – a tunnel that led to the outside world perhaps; and freedom! Thank you God! Thank you so very, very much.

You know, sometimes God plays nice!

Jones knocked on my bedroom door at precisely ten p.m. as arranged. He had two small torches, one each. He seemed much happier and smiled a wide toothy grin: his eyes didn't flicker quite as much: a load off his mind, it seemed.

We marched down the main corridor, past the laundry room, past the children's bedrooms, past The Queen's study, finally stopping outside my bathroom door.

"We're here," he announced as if I didn't know, and we stepped inside. I closed the door quietly behind us and went straight to the sink. It was surprisingly easy to locate the latch underneath the wash-hand basin and, just as in the previous night, the wooden panel slid noisily behind the toilet cistern.

I shone my light through the rectangular opening. Against the far wall was a mottled iron ladder, bolted on with ancient, rusty screws. This ladder descended a shaft as far as the eye could see and as I looked down a waft of putrid air rose to greet me. Bloody hell's fire, I thought; what a pong; smelly, disgusting and fantastic! I'm fourteen years-of-age, all over again.

"Well done, Jones; excellently well done. You shall know where to find me, if I go missing."

His smile instantly disappeared.

"Sir, I really don't think you should go on your own, I mean, a man in your position... what if you should... " He swallowed hard, his face blanching. "I also have a torch; we can descend together."

"Don't concern yourself Jones. If I go missing, the navy will pull out all the stops. If that fails, the army will be called; failing that, the air corps, civil defence, fire brigades, the AA, and every charity up and down the country, most of whom owe some form of allegiance. Failing all that, I'm sure Her Majesty will spare a corgi or two in the search."

He wasn't convinced by my light-heartedness: no sense of humour I'm afraid, but I ignored his reticence, exploded in laughter and slapped him hard on the back. I've discovered all my male staff love a good hefty smack on the back when they least expect it; only the males, you understand, and only on the back! Never had an objection, not one. Isn't that incredible? Does them good, I'm sure, like a bracing north-easterly at Balmoral.

"Now remember, not a word," I demanded, "not a word to anyone."

"Are you going now, sir?" he asked, his voice rising several octaves.

"No," I replied. "That would be foolhardy, would it not?"

"Yes sir, very sir, very indeed sir; no sir, don't go now sir."

"I agree with you, Jones. One must prepare properly for this type of expedition. I have read up on such like, you know. *The National Geographic* I find hugely informative. Only last week I read of a certain Captain Scott who undertook an exploration to the Antarctic and never came back. It would be a great shame, I think you'll agree, if the something similar happened to me."

He pondered this point for rather longer than was strictly

necessary. He was, no doubt, perplexed and a tad worried but in the end, he accepted the wisdom of my argument and off he went to bed.

When to go?

I decided there and then that this shaft, or whatever it was, would need exploring as soon as possible. Who knows where it might lead. I went to my room and checked the next day's work schedule.

Morning; nine-thirty a.m., Women's Institute with Her Majesty. State business at eleven-thirty; twelve-thirty, lunch with a Japanese delegation; investing in Britain… cars, lovely, can't possibly miss that! Afternoon; tea on the lawn with some scrubbed-up citizens; wonderful! Evening; Royal Variety, no wait… that's not until the next evening. Early nights all round at old Buck Palace, I'm sure. Superb! Opportunity knocks!

I thought it all through.

It made no difference what time of the evening I descended. Anne and Charles were back at school; boarded. Andrew and Edward in bed and Margaret, who knows? Her Majesty will opt for an early night, I decided: always did when there were no late engagements. That only left The Queen Mother. Unpredictable old bird, the queen mum. Loved nothing better than to saunter in to my quarters at any old time to offload a replay of the days racing: Kempton or Sandown or wherever; didn't knock! The winners she picked or didn't; Lester said this, Henry said that; farting machines, for all I cared… the horses, I mean. But one had to be careful not be rude, and to be fair, she did have a stable-full of horsey stories, some of them true. In any case, I asked her minder, Steven, where she would be. My luck was truly in. She was expected next day at Balmoral for some Scottish Highland flinging. So, early night guaranteed. Mission bathroom-tunnel was well and truly affirmative, green lighted, full steam ahead.

Picked up the flash light and tested the 'on' button. The batteries were fresh.

It was strangely satisfying to see one's family disappear in the mire

It may seem a trivial point and it had never occurred to me before but, what does one wear to explore an escape tunnel?

Worried about it all day. Distracted me. Old stuff, of course. Disposable, replaceable and most importantly… unimportant. Didn't want Her Majesty quizzing me on the strange odour from the good Aran sweater or the purple Pringle; no-no, and absolutely none of last year's Christmas presents. I simply needed a pair of old khakis and wellies, tattered jacket of some description and an old, worn jumper. I'd take a rucksack, fold-up walking stick, pen-knife, compass, banana and a long, long ball of string with a weight dangled at one end. A weight, yes, sensible; but what sort of weight? Came to me almost straight away: a royal paperweight, of course. Yes, one of those winter snow globes, with a music box underneath. They were everywhere about the palace; tripping over them; like rabbits in June. Wouldn't miss one, surely. The 'large', I thought, heavy, with all the family on the balcony; put the blasted thing to good use. And what would it be like, down the tunnel? Hot? Muddy? Smelly? Didn't want to overdress... or underdress: cold or sweltering? No way of knowing in advance. No idea. The thought occurred to me: meet a president, a dignitary; sorted in two minutes; morning suit, tuxedo, hair oil and shave, no problem, but send me down some stinky hole in the ground, now that's a challenge: what to wear? I was like a young lad hopping about; fretting, trying to get it right on a first date. Then again, I suppose it was a 'first date' of sorts.

I pulled the latch hard and jerked the door to the left. Damn, I thought, tight fit, but it moved with a little persuasion. A whiff of stale air rose to greet me. Pungent. Welcome change, though. Good honest pong. One last check; torch, pipe, rucksack; everything shipshape.

The ladder was attached to the far wall; iron construction; rusted but tightly screwed on and truly ancient; built to last. Hoped it was as sturdy as it seemed. Only one way to find out and I grabbed and yanked it from side to side. I could hear a grinding, crumbling sound from down below as one or two withered screws popped and disappeared somewhere down the shaft. Brick dust shot up. Hmmm, solid enough I supposed, and jumped on. Lit my pipe while I still had the bathroom light and shone the torch down the vertical shaft. Cripes. No bottom. This could be interesting. Slammed the door shut behind me. Deep breath; coughed; no turning back now.

I clambered down the ladder in darkness. Not too wobbly.

The pipe; bad idea. Completely forgot I would need my extra hand for the torch; easy mistake to make. No point in wasting the batteries till I got near the bottom so the torch stayed in my jacket pocket. My eyes began adjusting to the dark and the effort of being careful enough not to fall off or brush against the slimy tunnel walls began to heat me up. After the first hundred steps or so, I was perspiring profusely. The shaft was somewhat claustrophobic, being only just wide enough for a man of average build, but it was easy work, and my time in the navy, constantly skipping up and down ladders, was of great help. All of a sudden, after one hundred and fifty steps or so, I could make-out the bottom; just about. The ladder, despite my best efforts to dislodge, did its appointed duty and held the wall valiantly. Wondered who'd built it; darned fine effort.

The steps ended abruptly just four feet from the end, forcing me to jump off. My right welly landed in something very, very squelchy. Before I knew it, the ooze had seeped over the top and into the welly. Damn and blast; and the smell; noxious! I thought I was stuck for a moment, but fortunately, it only took just one hefty tug and I was free. I extinguished my pipe and switched on the torch.

A vast underground cavern appeared. I looked around slowly, taking it all in. Gloomy, sweaty, sticky and haunted by ten-thousand flickering, ghostly shadows, it seemed to expand in every direction, as far as the eye could see. Earth, stone, concrete and dirty, rust-covered pipes trailed away into the distance. Some of the ancient pipework had leaked from the ceiling, turning the ground beneath to a muddy sludge and the aged-blackened stonework, chiselled and chopped by some long-forgotten team of masons, stretched away in all directions. I took some time to look around and absorb this underground planet. The whole place had a strikingly eerie and lonely atmosphere and the vast, empty hollow was deadly quiet. It gave the impression of being untroubled by the outside world for years on end; barren and frozen in time beneath the opulent royal world directly above.

I raced my torchlight over the cowering darkness, making sure I did not miss any clues as to my new surroundings. One still needed to be careful. Fantastic, I enthused, wonderful; like camping out at Gordonstoun, only better, much, much, better! No superior to tell me what to do and no royal protocol to observe; a hidden kingdom on one's very own doorstep: one's very own middle earth.

I caught my breath for a second, then reached into the rucksack for the ball of string. The stillness was everywhere except for the occasional plop of water in a stagnant pool. I also took out my compass and looked for north. That was the plan, you see.

With my personal washroom close to the centre of the palace, and Green Park due north, I had calculated in advance that this was the direction one should explore first. I was unable say with any certainty, of course, but my gut instinct told me that if a concealed passage or tunnel leading to the outside existed, it was more likely to remain undiscovered beneath the park than beneath any of the major roads surrounding the palace. You follow my drift? The palace garden to the west was also an option but I reasoned that if I was to locate a tunnel in that direction, it might come up in the actual garden. What would one do then? I would still be trapped inside the palace walls. The roads beyond would have been constantly dug up, what with the advent of the tube, waterworks, drainage, cabling and the like, but Green Park or possibly St. James's Park would, hopefully, have remained relatively unmolested for many, many years. In any case, one had to start somewhere.

I looked down at the hole where my right welly had been. The black sludge was almost knee high. Might as well make use of it, I decided. I attached the string to the snow globe, winding it tight around the music box at the bottom end. I took a good look at the balcony scene before proceeding. Where was I? I wondered. Couldn't see myself; tying my shoelace perhaps? I then used my stick to shove the globe deep into the yielding slime. It was strangely satisfying to see one's family disappear into the mire on the end of a string, still smiling, still waving from the balcony; completely oblivious to their new-found occupation or indeed mine! From the depths of the sludge, the music box started up, all-be-it more than a little muffled;

God save our gracious Queen!
Long live our noble Queen! …

No time for sentiment; didn't wait till the end; off I went.

Step, squelch, step, squelch, I unravelled the ball as I went. The air was foul, like a hundred jock straps after a long day's batting on a dry wicket in Bangalore. The ceiling was low, maybe five feet, no more, so I was hunched over as I proceeded along. The whole thing was reminiscent of those

45

cobwebbed caves one sees in films, with anacondas and cockroaches and the like, except there probably weren't any; just muddy, smelly, putrid slime. I filled my lungs. Heaven was never this good. There were quite a few flies buzzing around. Where had they come from? Flies need food. I wondered what sustained them.

The way ahead was uncertain, both floor and ceiling uneven; undulating; damp. To make it more difficult, the foundations of the palace, for that's what they seemed to be, were also uneven; in some places, solid, stolid wall and stone structure, in other places practically non-existent, but with some sort of beam assembly to keep everything where it ought to be. The upshot was that one could not move in a straight line. I was moving in one direction, then suddenly forced to try another: first left then right, back and forth. Goodness knows, one could easily have ended-up totally lost without the string. I carried on for some time before checking my watch. Two-thirty a.m.; Tempis fugit, as my Latin teacher had often remarked back in the day, time to head back. I must have hiked three or four hundred yards, no more, but despite my best efforts I had to admit that, at half past two, time was against me. Had to be sensible, you know. Work tomorrow. Another notch in the annals of royal kow-towing needed to be struck whether I liked it or not. Black, belligerent mountains itching to assault a royal bedroom needed an actual royal, in his bed, to assault. I turned around and trudged back. My back ached and my feet ponged. Putrid!

Like a character from a fairy story, I gathered-in the string, wrapping it tight as I went; a slime-ball of congealed underworld. I pulled the paperweight from the mire. My

46

family popped out with a great slurp, still smiling, still waving; apparently pleased to see me. Up the ladder I went, much more slowly this time. At zero-two fifty-eight, precisely, I squeezed back through the hatch door. Down the corridor I crept, silent as a mouse with a squelchy welly, and straight to bed. The footwear, trousers, jumper and rucksack were flung in the far corner, beside an open window.

That night, for the first time in many months, I slept the sleep of the dead. Saint Peter bellowing from the gates of heaven would have had to give up and if Old Nick had taken me instead, he would have had to manhandle, step by step, my dilapidated, dead-weight corpse to the underworld, for I was, until next morning, beyond any form of resuscitation.

I knew I would suffer when I awoke, but it was worth it. Hadn't had such fun in a long, long time. Paid the price, let me tell you, and in full: discovered next morning what absolute exhaustion really meant!

10

I noticed the slightest twitching of her nose... here it comes

I hauled myself out of bed.

Everything ached, creaked and reeked. A neat bottle of Scotch would have inflicted less damage on my intestines. Below decks, on a hard bed, I had endured a sailor's discomfort; well used to it, but that was nearly twenty years earlier, when most of my body-hair was *above* my ears as opposed to *in* my ears. I smelt disgusting. My mouth harboured a dentist's nightmare and my sulking eyelids refused to open.

The valet stood over me.

"Quickly, sir, you've got to get up. Guests arriving in ten minutes and Her Majesty has already left for her opening."

"Yes, yes, all bloody right; no need to nag," I nagged; my tongue still worked.

I yawned a lungful and then several more. Even my lungs objected.

"Have you got my things? Who is it today? Is the shower running? Have I time to see the babies?"

Ah yes, the babies. Haven't mentioned them yet, have I? Late additions, you know: Andrew and Edward. Still so young. Wanted to see them more than time permitted. They needed to know who their father was, before it all became so very serious, too serious; spend parent time, important time, before they were whisked away by the morning bevy of nannies and pre-schoolers. I knew that, same as for Anne and Charles, time would march on. Mustn't neglect one's parental duties. No father should neglect his children, and here I was, damn it, doing just that. But, good lord; what could I do? Every bone ached, every muscle complained. Blasted tunnel. What possessed me?

"No sir, they're already at nursery."

The morning was long. I looked at my stubborn, skulking watch. It had a slimy black streak which extended over the face and across the strap, a memento of last night's exploits. The watch hung resentfully on my left wrist, refusing to tell me the right time. It told me the correct time, but not the right time. Twenty bloody minutes plodded by in the space of three bloody hours!

I love the WWF, make no mistake: course I do; great organisation and vital for the future of the planet but my enthusiasm for this most worthy of causes, had been lost in the slipstream of the previous night's adventure. I distinctly remember the beginning of the nine-thirty meeting; everyone was there, all scrubbed up, perfumed, manicured; slimeless watches. The president, committee members and secretaries were all in attendance. Hands were shaken, agendas issued, policy discussed and plans presented. We all nodded vigorously as if trying to achieve an Olympic qualifying mark.

'Greater visibility' someone said, and we all agreed, though in truth, my own was decidedly limited at that point. Book launch, interviews for the Beeb, the world service; that's the ticket. I remember needing more coffee than usual. My equerry was brilliant: prods in the back, digs in the ribs and a kick to my left shin under the table, which was totally uncalled for... but necessary; kept me awake, clever boy. Cannot remember the detail. I'm sure I proposed something appropriate; one always does. Something equally appropriate was, I'm sure, counter-proposed for further discussion and approval, and so on and so forth, until all appropriate proposals had been appropriately proposed, discussed, and approved, as they always are. I remember having a pen shoved in my hand and one feels certain something important was signed. I know it was important because there were more than the usual number of emblems and inscriptions in my peripheral vision. Top quality paper was used, I noticed, not the cheap stuff. Assembled guests held their collective breath, lest I be unable to complete my name.

Beyond that, nothing.

Couldn't keep my eyes open for all the tea in China. I might have been authorising the beginning of a new opium war, for all I knew, but I spelled Philip correctly, in the good Queen's English and that seemed to satisfy them. The wild-lifers went away happy. At the stroke of a pen, hippos, orang-utans, and gorillas had been saved from extinction, though I myself could have gone either way. Flipside of adventure, you know; there's always a flipside; same in the navy... exhaustion!

Etched in my mind from the early afternoon following the morning after the night before, was the silence of Her Majesty.

We met for an official lunch, she back from slicing a sacrificial ribbon or smashing a blameless bottle and I, straight down from the WWF. She is excellent, always has been, at pointing out the minutiae of my indiscretions and lapses. I mean that positively. Heaven knows I need all the help I can get. I rely on her to advise me on personal presentation issues: the straightness of tie, the shine of shoe, the impeccability of one's cuffs and the stiffness of one's collar. Nothing; she had nothing to say. Her hands were clasped, her shoulders slightly slung back, rigid, and her lips, tight. She said nothing. I was in trouble. She smiled warmly for the press. She can't know... surely not! She acknowledged the excellent work done. She'd had an early night, I know she had! A wonderful achievement, she beamed at the expectant guests. All my muddy stuff from beside the open window would have been taken away early, so it can't have been that. "Thank you for your kindness," she proffered before shooting an icy eye in my direction. Then I noticed the slightest twitching of her nose. The guests had disappeared, the press dispatched. Here it comes!

"Where were you Philip?"

That evening we entertained a Chinese delegation and I was much recovered. I have always had fond regard for the Chinese and their tea. Indeed I have fond regard for visiting dignitaries of all nations who produce something worth drinking; love the Scots and the Irish, but the Chinese I really like. I think it's because we understand each other so well. I understand their culture and they understand my humour. I have simply lost count of the number of times an ambassador or wife have waited with bated breath, mouth slightly agape, waiting for one's next astute observation; same as the press, really. Appearance, culture, diet etc., but most of all, I appreciate their ability to join in the humour, the jolly banter. Everyone loves them, you know, my little asides; especially the Chinese; language no barrier.

"Where was I? What do you mean Elizabeth?"

"Andrew and Edward were in the breakfast room until eight-fifteen. Really Philip, you must make an effort. No doubt up too late taking-in the wildlife of Borneo or somewhere, or down a *National Geographic* cave with a flashlight."

Oh good heavens! Did she know something?

"Well yes, I mean no, I mean, of course, Elizabeth… and yes, yes absolutely, one must set one's clock for earlier. I did want to darling, you know I did, but… "

"Well you had better, Philip. We rarely see you on time for breakfast and now, you're neglecting our children, especially after you said you would try to be… improved."

Dressing down.

Her Majesty delivers the best. I should know. I'm normally at the receiving end and as I stood there, yet again, I found myself listening to the busy hum of her exasperated tones. I looked down at my patent leather shoes and could not help but marvel at the superb shine; must complement the footman; could see myself clearly in both shoes at the same time; first one then the other, impeccable shine;

fascinating! Laces all done up...? Yes... good... oops; a pause. Her Majesty had momentarily stopped, awaiting my contrition.

"Yes dear, sorry dear."

She continued and I had time to notice a biggish claret-like stain under my left foot. Spilled bottle of red? I wondered. No... not quite wide enough. Probably no more than half a glass, perhaps not wine at all; might have been... what else is red? Beetroot salad or a strawberry sundae... or perhaps something furry a corgi might have brought in from the garden, dripping... wait, wait... she's slowing down... almost to a halt; my turn again. One final apology should do it.

"Please forgive me Elizabeth... I... I really am most dreadfully sorry... "

There's a break, a silence. As predicted, I sense the end. After eighteen years, one becomes... attuned. She exhales and relaxes, then, almost casually, sniffs the air.

"What's that smell...? Can you get it, Philip? It's coming from... is it your socks? Your sleeve, your watch I think; the strap. Look, there's a great, black, smelly smear Philip. Get it off! Good heavens. And you look a bit peaky. Are you coming down with something? What's that in your eye? Let me see."

A royal handkerchief was produced and put to good use extracting a small section of eyeball. I winced, she smiled and I was back in the good books.

11

"MI5 and MI6 have been fully informed, and MI7 shall, if it ever comes into existence"

Over the next few weeks, one gradually found an hour here and there to descend the depths and continue the exploration. Had to be devious, of course and daring.

I remembered a night during the war, when my ship, the *Wallace*, was in imminent danger from the dive-bombing Stukas. We created a diversion and slipped away under cover of darkness: set fire to a decoy raft. Marvellous ploy and it worked very, very well! We escaped! Never forgot that lesson. Diversion: that's the key.

A little deviousness: nothing at all wrong with that; nothing too outrageous, of course. We have our principles do we not? Just enough to create a little space in which to abscond unnoticed. Naturally I did not wish to cause unnecessary concern with my necessary absences.

"Need to pop over to St James's to meet the Home Secretary, dear. Shan't be long."

"Did I forget to mention the dentist today? How forgetful of me."

"Barber, darling: look at the length of my hair!"

"As I'm free this afternoon, perhaps I should avail of the opportunity to do some study, darling."

Then the dash began: a tunnel to explore.

Quickly into the jungle gear. Over to the bathroom, quietly, of course. Sometimes ran a bath… with the plug out! Great tactic, that. Plenty of noise; no metering in those days. Unlatch the hidden panel and off I went. Quite soon, even if I say so myself, I excelled at transforming from smiling consort in Her Majesty's kingdom one minute, to explorer of my own personal underground kingdom the next… and no-one suspected a thing. Well, when I say 'no-one', that's not quite true. The butler, Jones, knew. One could see he was clearly unhappy at my 'unusual' absences. They were, after all, facilitated by him, in that, he had found the escape passage in the first place and had passed it along to me, so-to-speak. In a court of law, he could easily have found himself thundered at by a learned judge:

"And did you not, Mr Jones, unlawfully and without legal or royal precedent, wilfully allow Prince Philip, The Duke of Edinburgh, herein after called, 'The Victim', to descend the shaft, herein after called 'The Tunnel of Death', thereby allowing him, 'The Victim', by your gross negligence, opportunity to cause himself the utmost harm, leading

to his slow, agonising, painful, and tortuous death by starvation, with nothing but an overripe banana and a snow globe of his family, to sustain him during his final, desperate, hours?"

His needs or mine? I questioned; his or mine? Tough one. Mine of course!

The monarchy, as represented by me, prevailed. Far more important, I think you'll agree, the needs of one's country and of one's Commonwealth.

Several times he had found himself protecting my non-availability: a phone call would come through, or one of the children would ask him why I was taking so long in the bath *and* in the middle of the afternoon, or The Queen would send for me… this and that. Jones found himself to be 'keeper of the consort's absence', a position he neither asked for nor wanted, and one which would never result in a New Year's Honours listing or even a modest pay rise. Whenever I saw him, he appeared in a state of panic. He seemed always to be mopping his brow, even on the coldest of days. I feared he would crack and spill the beans, so one evening, late, I sent for him.

"Have a seat, Mr Jones."

"Thank you, sir."

"I want you to know how pleased I am with your… butlering… and Her Majesty, of course, not just me. We are both astonishingly pleased with the upmost care and attention lavished on the various items, em, requiring attention. The silverware is beyond reproach… and the crockery; spotless. One checks one's reflection in your spoons almost on a daily basis … and with very pleasing results."

56

"Thank you again, sir."

"But, I notice you appear to be under some degree of, how should one put it…? Stress."

"You'll kill yourself, sir!"

"Pardon?"

"Sure as eggs are eggs sir, you'll find yourself dead if you keep this up, sir."

"Now, now Jones, perspective please; you worry too much… "

"But you will sir and I'll be held responsible, and The Queen will probably bring back the hanging sir, just for me, mark my words. You'll die down there and I'll be strung up, up here, over there at The Tower sir, because I could have said something to someone but said nothing about anything to nobody sir, and I'll get the blame and I don't know what to do or even if there's something I should do sir, because I might be the cause of… "

"Wait, wait, wait," I said, "you're panicking man. Pull yourself together… "

"I've seen the state of your clothes, sir, all smelly and dirty. It must be shocking down there… filthy. Maybe we should, I mean the footmen, valets and myself, do some overtime and go down with you to clean the place up while you do your adventuring sir. I'd feel much better… "

"No, Jones, no. No one must know; no one. Do I make myself clear?"

He fell silent and I pondered; eventually deciding to tell the tiniest white lie, distort the truth by the merest fraction.

"You see… it's a security issue. What you're not aware of is that I have decided to conduct a personal survey of the security arrangements beneath the palace. Top secret, you understand… code… ninety-nine, and you and I, together, must put the monarchy ahead of our own personal concerns. Do you understand?"

Before he had time to digest this new information I forged ahead.

"MI5 and MI6 have been fully informed, and MI7 shall, if it ever comes into existence: the three 'M's, as we refer to them, Her Majesty and I. We must coordinate the under-the-palace security network to ensure the continued safety of all the very, very valuable people we have working and living here, for all of our collective benefit and for the benefit of our great country, and indeed the entire Commonwealth… don't you think?"

"Well… yes sir."

I had him now.

"The invisibility of the work I have undertaken, underground, to protect the necessary viability and integrity of the monarchy as a whole, is undeniably vital, you'll agree, and will undoubtedly vindicate the aptly applied initiatives already instigated and implemented, don't you think?"

His eyes had glazed over.

"So are we agreed, Mr Jones: absolute silence. The nation needs butlers like you… silent ones."

He nodded then stood and walked towards the door.

"One other matter, sir, beg your pardon. Do you think I could have a pay rise next year?"

"At a time of national crisis? Course not. We're not the Bank of England, you know!" And I sent him on his way with a flea in his ear.

Cheek of him, trying to pull a fast one like that!

12

A pair of Quasimodos eyed each other in the gloom

I'd had an excellent run; diversions working a treat. Jones had fallen into line without a squeak, though one did find oneself routinely casting him a jaundiced eye lest he forget our 'understanding'. Opportunities for burrowing were popping up faster than cock pheasants on a summer shoot.

Tough decisions ensued.

My study or tunnel...? Tunnel.

Additional royal duties or tunnel...? Tunnel.

Extra play time with one's children or tunnel…? Ashamed to say but tunnel.

Late evening walk in the garden with Her Majesty or tunnel…?

Walk in the garden, of course. One may be an idiot but one is not stupid!

Problem was, I was making no progress. You see, I couldn't seem to find a way forward. I would dash down, anchor the string securely, unravel and away, but I would either run out of time or end up facing a brick wall... quite literally, an ancient brick wall! I was becoming frustrated with this damned impasse when I took the decision, on a Thursday, four fifty-five p.m. precisely, to head off due east instead of due north as I had been doing. Hopefully I would find a route towards The Queen Victoria Memorial and from there swing ninety degrees north, as originally planned. Pointless adopting tactics that simply weren't working!

I sloshed and slogged my way along, all the time hunched beneath the low ceiling.

Fifty paces out, as I unwound the string for the umpteenth time, I noticed something quite extraordinary. There was a pile of newspapers on my left, stacked neat against a dry brick wall. Over I went. *Evening Standard*s, the lot. I picked up the top copy and shone the torch. Very recent... May 27th nineteen sixty-six. Well, well, I thought, how odd. I found somewhere to sit and quickly leafed through the pages. Usual stuff on the front page: The Queen this, Charles that, Anne the other. No sign of me! What else? Hippies, drugs, The Rolling Stones – stoned. Read my horoscope, a small weakness of mine; page twenty-eight, Gemini; 'You will feel down, today but help will arrive when least expected'. Rubbish. And on the back page, 'Bobby Moore to lift the Cup'. What cup? I wondered. No time to read. Had work to do.

I looked again at the pile. Must have been five hundred of them just lying there, neatly. The silence, up to now quite pleasant, suddenly became intimidating. Was it the heat? I felt the merest trickle of perspiration on the back of my neck. I was alone or was I? Could there be someone else down here, watching, perhaps waiting? Obviously somebody had been down here, and recently. I listened intently… nothing. I shone the torch slowly all around taking more care than ever. Not a dicky-bird.

Footprints; I'll check for footprints.

There were a few in the mud and they looked like mine, but on closer inspection, I could see I was mistaken. There were two distinct sets, the size and shape of the second set clearly different. These prints, I could see, took off in a southerly direction and from where I stood, quickly disappearing into the murk. I had never been to the south side. Again I peered into the darkness. The silence was suddenly deafening.

Was I alone?

Idiot nincompoop, of course not! *Evening Standard*s don't stack themselves, do they? I realised I was alone in someone else's domain; had to be; alone and vulnerable.

By now, it really was hot. I pulled off my woolly jumper and fanned myself with a *Standard*. My shirt clung to me and I dabbed a dampening brow. It took all my resolve to retain my composure. Despite all evidence, I found it difficult to convince myself that some other person not only walked these underground caverns but apparently enjoyed nothing better than a good read in the afternoon. But equally, one felt such a fool thinking that one could, or indeed should, be the only visitor to the palace underground. None of these musings helped solve my problem.

What to do?

I took several deep lungfuls of stagnant air to mull it over. One or two of those annoying flies came by to inspect. I made a decision: with hindsight a decidedly bad one given my lack of preparedness, but in any case, I decided not to investigate the offending footprints or to venture back to the safety of the shaft. One must be resolute, I concluded; one must follow one's predetermined plan.

Decision made, I continued eastwards, unravelling as I went, and acutely aware I was much more on edge than before, listening for any sign of a fellow burrower, watching-out for a would-be assailant, or even, heaven forbid, a would-be assassin. The shadows became darker, the mud deeper; the flashlight dimmer. I began to squint, but I soldiered on.

At five twenty-five, p.m., I turned a promising corner but instead of the hoped-for escape exit, I came up against yet another massive barrier of bricks and mortar. There was no way forward. My neck ached from the constant stooping. Too late, I thought. Enough for today. Nothing to do but retrace my steps, wind in the string and re-join the living world upstairs. I took out my banana, about to peel.

"Your Highness, I presume."

"What?"

"Your Royal Highness, Prince Philip; may I be of assistance?"

A man's figure, hunched over, had ghosted into view, right arm extended and I slammed the back of my head hard on the ceiling.

"Are you all right, sir?"

"Who the hell are you? What's going on? Stay back, I warn you!"

For a moment a pair of Quasimodos eyed each other in the gloom. I took a step back and raised my banana hand. I left him in no doubt I had fruit and was prepared to use it.

"I'm trying to help you sir."

"Who are you?"

"The Earl of Buckingham, sir, at your service."

He might have been a maniac: deranged. Why else would he be down here? Only later did it occur to me just how ironic that thought was. I had to act quickly. Might be dangerous; perhaps armed, even better than I. But he was calm and appeared to be behaving rationally so I decided to acquiesce… for the moment, at least. He stood waiting for my next move.

"Well, Mr... Buckingham, thank you for your kind offer, but as you can see, I've taken care to lay down some string with which to find my way back, so thank you but no thank you."

I almost shook his hand.

"You're bleeding, Highness."

"You can't speak to me like that… oh, you mean blood, well yes, but just a little… ouch… oh yes, it does hurt."

"This way sir. I have sticking plaster and iodine."

He turned and walked away in the dark, clearly expecting me to follow. I followed his expectation. What else could I have been expected to do? It was clear he knew his way around, not needing a torch and that. He was in control and I felt it would have been in vain to challenge. Besides he had, I was assured, some sticking plaster... and iodine.

We carried on until we came to a door, a normal wooden door, but shorter. What the hell? I thought, a door, here? It was squashed between ceiling and floor and opened inwards; reminded me of a hobbit's. He flicked a switch and a light came on... electric light... down here? Was I paying for this? Hmmm, I thought, but said nothing.

"Please sit down sir," he ushered.

The light blinded me for a moment but when I held my hand up, adjusting to the brightness, I could see I was standing in some rudimentary sitting room; proper sized. Must have been at least twenty five feet long and almost as wide. The floor was beneath the level of the door, so that it was possible to stand up straight.

"Over here, sir," he said and pointed to a plush but ancient armchair; worn purple velvet covering, with a rug draped across the back. I did as I was told, stretching as I went. A neat bump had risen on top of my head, but the blood had stopped.

The armchair was very comfortable.

The Earl, if that's what he really was, went over to a cupboard and began looking for something, presumably the first-aid box. Well, well, well, I thought. Who would have believed it? Living quarters underneath the palace.

I twisted and stretched and relieved my aching limbs as best I could and looked around. There was carpet on the floor and wood panelling on the walls. Everything looked ancient, smelt of moth balls and was decidedly tatty. The stench was here too, fusty, but not quite as bad as outside. The light was too dim to see clearly but being a guest, I chose not to point out this minor inadequacy. I could see a kitchen area to my left and stretching away to my right was a hallway through which several partially-hidden doors were visible. Incredible,

I thought, utterly unbelievable, a *Standard*-reading underground Earl in his own little underground palace… amazing indeed.

Upstairs, little did I know, but a very different scenario was unfolding.

13

Those astonishing eyes are my very own eyes

"In eighteen years, he has never gone missing, not once; never been out of view nor misplaced in all that time. One has always found him wherever one has left him; that's the key with Philip. Give him clear, precise instructions and he will always obey: the navy training, you know. Most distressing, most. Utterly unlike him to vanish without saying."

Her Majesty takes out her handkerchief and dabs each eye in turn. She sobs, sniffles, blows and worries.

"He left at four-thirty, saying he would be in his study: likes to delve into his hobbies, you see: religion, God, the meaning of life, that sort of thing, and of course his other favourites: flowers and trees, mostly. Then there's the tigers, lions, baboons and so forth, for the WWF. He's preserving them for the future along with Prince Bernhard. How often did I hear him say I also had a duty to look after each and every dumb animal and now he's gone."

Her Majesty sobs again. Large tears roll down her face, her eyes glistening, her hands clasped. The officers look at each other not exactly sure what to do. Often a female officer will comfort a member of the public by placing a sympathetic arm around a shoulder, but this is The Queen. If an arm were to be placed on a royal shoulder, the officer in question could leave herself open to a charge of 'improper comforting'. At the very least, promotion prospects would be seriously jeopardised. Fortunately, a passing Lady-in-Waiting assists, allowing Her Majesty to sigh and sob with appropriate propriety.

Officers Major and Brown had been having their early evening break when the call came through. Naturally they had rushed over, despite Her Majesty's protestation that she wished to be treated as an ordinary citizen. The on-duty sergeant, PC Steven Major, fortunately recognising the seriousness of the situation, had barely enough time to finish-off his ham, cheese and pickle sandwich, on brown, before gulping a second medium-sized coffee and devouring his favourite afternoon treat: a fruit scone with a creamy nutmeg and cinnamon filling. He pays a quick visit to the gents before leaving, checking hair, teeth and straightness of cap. Must be presentable for The Queen! Then dashing directly to the palace, he leaves strict instruction that nobody take *his* spare scone from the fridge. In the car, WPC Brown double-checks the address and applies lipstick.

They hurry through the gates of the palace and straight to

Her Majesty's quarters, A tearful Queen relates the afternoon's events.

"He's simply gone; vanished!"

"There's no need to be alarmed, Your Majesty," PC Major says. "I'm sure there's a perfectly rational explanation for your husband's abduction."

"Abduction?"

"Too early to tell Ma'am, but the good news is that royal hostages are normally returned, intact, within two to three months. On the other hand, Your Majesty, if he has been unfortunate enough to fall into a well or from, say, a roof, he has a smaller chance of survival but we tend to find the body quicker. It's never all bad news."

"Body!"

Her Majesty again avails of her handkerchief. Ladies-in-Waiting rush over. Corgis yap.

The door bursts open and The Queen Mother, accompanied by Princes Charles, Andrew and Princess Anne, arrive looking worried. Baby Edward is carried in by his nursery nurse, mercifully oblivious to the unfolding tragedy. An equerry and the butler follow behind, heads bowed. The Queen hugs her children, as never before. WPC Paula Brown draws a deep breath and comforts the siblings.

"Now don't you worry, young ones. I'm sure your dear father will be found alive and well, unless he's dead."

PC Major has opened his briefcase on a side table underneath a stern portrait of Queen Mary. He carefully pulls out a file of A4 sheets labelled 'Missing Persons' and looks to his colleague for assistance.

"What does the white one say, Brown, and the blue?"

"The white says 'Members of the Public' and the blue, 'Persons of Special Interest'."

"So it's neither of those. What about the green?"

"Clergy, Politicians and Foreigners."

"OK, that's a maybe. Anything else in the file; look, there's an off-colour at the bottom… the cream; what does that one say?"

"Royalty and/or Criminals, sir."

"Ah yes, that's the one."

PC Major takes out a pen and a clipboard and sits beside Her Majesty. The family pull up some chairs and form a semi-circle of support.

"We need to collect some information, Ma'am. Nice easy one to start: name?"

"Philip."

"Thank you. Ethnic origin? You'll need to think carefully, Your Majesty; them upstairs are getting very fussy about this one."

"German… no Greek… no British… yes British. He used to be a foreigner but he's one of us now."

"Recent photograph, in case… for the officers at the station to circulate."

Her Majesty looks around. There's nothing on the walls.

"Charles, try the desk in the corner. Anne, I think we have some family snaps in albums upstairs. Be an angel and bring them down, dear. Andrew, you can help Anne. There's a good boy. Jones, I have some stamps in the two old biscuit tins, in the kitchen. Could you fetch them for me, please?"

She nods at the butler who hurries to obey.

Her Majesty is slightly more composed.

"If we can't find any good snaps of him, one may find him on a stamp, though I have to admit, it is mostly me these days. Would you like some tea?"

"I think not, Ma'am. It's vital we proceed with utmost speed... well maybe half a cup, two sugars and a good dash. Now where was he last seen?"

The Queen sits back.

"He was on his way to the study at half past four... "

She looks at her watch. It's almost eight-thirty p.m.

"One has had no husband for nearly four hours." And she sobs again but this time with a more regal composure. "That's where he said he was going... oh heavens above, where can he be?"

The butler arrives with the boxes of stamps which he hands to The Queen. She rummages through the first box, labelled 'Keeps', looking for any of her husband.

"Me, me, me," she mumbles, shaking her head in disappointment. "Oneself and birds, oneself and buildings, oneself and dignitaries." The Queen continues flicking stamps left and right in exasperation. "No, nothing here," she declares to no one in particular. She opens the second box, labelled 'Swops'. Again she carefully trawls through the, mostly, used stamps, but, again, to no avail. "Just oneself and important people, so he won't be here. Ah, Charles, what have you got? Let me see."

She sorts the various photos of herself, extended royalty, family and politicians.

"Oh here's one," she exclaims hopefully and holds it up. "Oh no, he's pointed the wrong way and he's half behind Anne's pony." Finally The Queen Mother speaks.

"That nice Mr. Beaton did a black and white for his passport, a few weeks ago. Do you remember? Does it for a job, you know. It's in the official satchel for your approval. I think it should suffice, dear."

The Queen looks perplexed.

"Mother. Do you mean my *private* official satchel? Surely you haven't…"

"Just a hunch, dear, how should I know?"

Sergeant Major agrees that passport photos will be more than adequate. He carefully picks up his cup, stirs it thoroughly then slowly sips, appreciating a quality brew rarely available at the station. He adds a little extra sugar and a thimbleful of milk. There are no biscuits so he turns to The Queen.

"Shall we carry on, Ma'am? There's no time to lose."

"Hair colour and style?"

"Blond and short."

"And height, please Ma'am?"

"Six feet and one inch."

"Eyes, Your Majesty?"

"Wonderful, sergeant." Her voice becomes a whisper. "Those eyes are the reason why I fell in love so totally, so very deeply. Can you image such intensity, sergeant…? Such purpose, such power, yet gentle, warm and supportive. Over the many years all one has needed to do was look; look and see the exquisite man behind the façade. No matter how alone I felt, he was always there. Sometimes I wanted to run, to shirk my duty. Sometimes he wanted to run but together we were and still are steadfast; performing our duties, honouring our commitments and will continue to do so for as long as we both shall live. Those astonishing eyes are my very own eyes and will remain so as long as I am Queen to my people, wife to my husband and mother to my children. Only God can… "

"I meant the colour, Ma'am."

"Blue."

The sergeant stands up and clears his throat. He takes a few steps towards the window, all the time checking his paperwork and considering his next move.

"That's the written work done, Ma'am. I think it's important we place your husband's disappearance in the public domain as a matter of some urgency. The sooner we have the public on our side, the easier it will be to retrieve him for you; a press release of some description, maybe a small classified in the *Horse and Hound*.."

Prince Charles nods and Princess Anne sheds a quiet tear. The Queen Mother also concurs, with a whimsical nod. The butler eyes a 'told-you-so' towards the equerry, but The Queen, again becoming tearful, strongly dissents.

"Oh no, one simply cannot do that. What will the people think, the Commonwealth? No, much too risky. One's subjects may speculate in ways totally unbecoming their sovereign and leap to all manner of conclusion. Shall we tell the press that a royal has gone missing, but not specify which one? Best of both worlds. We shall have one's subjects looking, but they shan't know who they're looking for."

"Yes, yes, Your Majesty; what an excellent plan. We shall draft the 'missing persons' description along those lines." He tilts his head back and rubs his chin.

"Brown, write this down."

MISSING PERSONS PRESS RELEASE:
POPULAR MEDIA AND THE BBC.

ONE ROYAL
SIX FEET AND ONE INCH
BLUE EYES
BLOND
POSSIBLY BRITISH
ANYONE FOUND MATCHING THIS
DESCRIPTION TO BE RETURNED
TO BUCKINGHAM PALACE IMMEDIATELY

14

Service sir, but not as you know it

As I looked across the room, the Earl of Buckingham, for that's what he insisted on being called, came over with a bottle of iodine, a swab of cotton and a whopping great sticking plaster.

"Hold still, Your Royal Highness," he said, "this may sting a little."

Certainly made sure any germs were taken care of and a sizeable portion of my scalp, to boot. My head stung like a nest of angry wasps and I stank of iodine to the high heavens. He then wandered over to the drinks cabinet.

"I really must go," I insisted, but before I rose he thrust a ten-year-old single malt in my hand. Dashing away would have been unkind. One must endeavour not to fly in the face of such civility, so reluctantly I accepted his hospitality, and equally reluctantly, several more over the course of the next hour or so. I looked around his sitting room.

There was a table and chairs, and a television in the far corner. Very cosy! To my left was a display cabinet with lots of ghastly plastic trinkets, the sort of thing dear old grandmama would collect on a trip to the seaside; absolutely dreadful plastic tat with not a shred of value. Carrying on around the room, there were paintings on every wall. I recognised most, if not all of what was on display. A wedding photo of Elizabeth and me; the children on the west lawn – how did he get that? – one or two of the navy vessels on which I had served: The *Ramillies*, the *Kent*, unless I was mistaken, the *Shropshire* and the *Valiant*. To my right and at my back were portraits of me at different ages; as a boy in Paris, then in full navy uniform and yet more of me escorting The Queen on her public duties and finally, me, yet again, in full cricket attire. I was truly amazed, astonished, I must say; an excellent collection! But where was his family? Not a sign. Strange, I thought and more than a little sad. I carried on around the walls, arriving back at the display cabinet with its many plastic trinkets, some of which were quite tasteful indeed.

"It's such a pleasure, Your Highness, to finally make your acquaintance."

"I really must go… "

" … after all these years of service to the royal household," he continued.

"Service?"

"Service sir, but not as you know it, Royal Household Security, MI5."

"What? MI what?"

"I'm sure it must come as a shock sir, but it was decided to keep this entire operation secret. Nobody knows of the underground palace except MI5, the prime minister and now you."

Amazed, aghast and quite frankly appalled, I sat there, dumbfounded.

"Not even The Queen?"

"No sir."

"Stop, stop," I insisted. "One is not sure one should be hearing all of this."

"With respect, Your Highness, it's too late now," he countered. "We're in this together… have a top-up sir, one for the ladder."

Great Scott! I thought, what have I done? but surprisingly, just one or two glasses later, my concerns had been somewhat allayed. The whisky was superb. Best I've ever had; probably the storage. We chatted for quite a while but he was reluctant to divulge the details of the operation. Just as well. I was equally reluctant to hear, so we indulged in inconsequential small talk; holidays, the weather etc. etc. Must have been ten p.m. when I finally struggled to the base of the shaft. The Earl had taken me back. Seemed like a decent chap, all told, despite my reservations.

"I shall be in touch, sir," he said. "There's more to see, in due course."

I abandoned my wellies, which ponged with some gusto, and climbed the ladder in stocking feet; out through the hidden panel and into the bathroom. I knew instinctively I would have been missed, so had to come up with an alibi credible enough to get me off the hook. I checked the way was clear and tip-toed back to my bedroom. Once there, I crawled underneath the bed and let out the most enormous groan. Within thirty seconds feet clambered from every direction. Crawling out from underneath, my relieved family, staff and police hailed my return and breathed a collective sigh of relief. Surely somebody had checked? They had checked the entire palace and I was under my own bed! However, it was very dark underneath and I had all sorts stored there: boots, luggage cases, unopened gifts from the most recent three or four state dinners, lost underwear, missing socks, pocket battleships, etc. etc.; easy to miss a royal curled up having banged his head and passed out. Paper thin of course, my alibi, but nobody dared question the veracity of my story or, indeed, the smell of whisky from my breath, the yellow bump on my scalp or my sludge-covered stockings; nobody! Advantages to being a royal, you know. Sometimes it's good to be, if not the king, then the consort; one's own little bit of power you know; muscle. Lucky escape though, and plenty to think about. I would need to be better prepared next time and finding out I had a titled hermit living underneath the palace was more than a little unnerving. Did I really want to continue with the lies and deception? Could 'the Earl' be trusted? What to do?

Over the next few weeks, one had to be patient.

I waited for the message from below. The Earl would contact me: that's what he'd said and I decided, in the absence of a more advantageous plan, to comply. Yes, one could have made the descent, continued to explore, but having seen some of the palace below, I realised I was a total amateur with my bananas and my string. There was something more serious going on and I had to be patient in finding out exactly what. So I contented myself with the knowledge that contact would be made in due course, and I would, thereafter, be in a better position to continue or otherwise.

Life carried on, while I waited. Usual stuff; this and that. I remember, my darling wife had something on her mind.

"Crufts," she announced.

"Beg your pardon Elizabeth."

"Crufts, dear. I'm thinking of entering a dog next year. Should stand a good chance of winning, don't you think? You know what I like in a dog; one only keeps the best: impeccable breeding, good natured, indisputable lineage and instant obedience. You simply must agree with me Philip."

I agreed, of course and she went away happy, but I'm not sure if she ever did in the end… so long ago.

Tedious stuff too. Even we royals have to do the mundane, you know, and I'm pleased to say Elizabeth was quite happy to squeeze in her share of the household administration.

"I've renewed the insurances, Philip."

"Well done my dear; another job out of the way."

"Quite fortuitous, really; all very smooth for a change."

"Well done, darling."

"But most unusual, Philip. I awoke yesterday morning and there was a strange man sitting on my bed. Said he'd tried to phone but kept getting fobbed off… my secretary would not put him through. So he exercised his initiative, so he said, in much the same way as you used to do Philip, and scaled the wall; shimmied up the drainpipe and into my room. Well, I could hardly turn him away after all that effort but best of all, he did the lot, there and then while we were in the bed together: palaces, castles, houses, horses, the lot; full no claims

78

bonus to boot and contents! Fortunately, I had my chequebook beside the bed. One feels so much safer now, Philip, having been so comprehensively covered."

"What a stroke of luck that was, Elizabeth! Does he do carriages?"

Time kicked on. Still hadn't heard from the Earl and I grew anxious.

There were engagements and meetings, state dinners and private receptions; Lords and Headingly, Ascot and Epsom not to mention the royal trips home and abroad; domestic life. Weeks became months. Nothing from underground… silence. On one occasion my lack of patience almost got the better of me and I went as far as opening the hidden panel. I stared down the shaft into the darkness but stopped short, like an addict facing down his own addiction. At night I dreamt of freedom and fresh air, of big, big ships and bright billowing sails over a vast blue ocean. But the old demons also returned, stronger than ever. Black belligerent mountains pressed hard on the window panes, waiting for me, pushing at me, impatient, trying to break me, each and every morning, even as I tried so hard to purge them from my head. I had to get out.

Thursday afternoon, early October, and Jones, the butler, handed me an afternoon paper. This was unusual. I only ever took the morning *Telegraph*, but when I saw it was an afternoon *Standard*, I knew this was the call. Jones nodded and looked away. Written in the margin of the front page were the five numbers; three, fourteen, fifteen, twenty-two and twenty three. Some sort of code, I deduced. It was simple. I looked at each page in turn and picked out the single underlined word on each, which I wrote down in succession.

'Tonight', 'there', 'p.m'., 'ten' and 'be'.

What could they mean? I was never good at puzzles. Did quite well to find the pages.

'There be ten p.m. tonight'. Hmmm. But there's ten p.m. every night: ridiculous. 'p.m. tonight ten be there' I'm to meet the Prime Minister at ten, but where? Good heavens.

I'm not ashamed to say, I was struggling. Finally, when I had almost given up, Jones came over and whispered in my ear.

"Ten p.m. tonight, be there", and he pointed downwards. Well, well, well, I thought with more than a little satisfaction; useful to have a clued-in butler.

"Thank you, Jones."

No engagements tonight, perfect; but of course the Earl already knew this… and Jones too, it would seem. Can you imagine my surprise? Until now, I had thought of Jones as an unwilling participant in my endeavours to escape. But now I realised it was all an act, a ruse, to make sure I was capable of keeping a secret. Jones was also MI5, had to be! Both he and the Earl together, in cahoots. But what was their agenda, their purpose?

Perhaps I would have an answer later that night.

15

Faster than a rash over a bouncing baby's bottom

Slipped the latch, slid-open the panel and down the ladder.

One had to reacquaint oneself with the underworld. Had quite forgotten just how foul the air was; the slimy walls and the smothering mud; flies everywhere. Jumped off the bottom rung. Nobody there. Waited ten minutes in the dark for the Earl to emerge. One is not used to being kept waiting. I was rapidly becoming annoyed. I considered yelling a greeting of some sort, but thought the better of it. Finally I could wait no longer. I decided to make my way over to his abode, the underground palace. Taking out my trusty royal paperweight and making sure the string was securely fastened, I plunged it into the mud pile and took off eastbound for the underground palace, all the time on the look-out for my tardy host. After approximately ten minutes or so, I arrived at the door of his living quarters. Curiosity got the better of me and instead of knocking, I decided to carry on for a bit, to see what was around the far side, unravelling as I went. Another altogether narrower door than the Earl's appeared in the murk; planks of aged wood nailed together, but sturdy. There was no lock, just an old Bakelite knob which opened easily on a first turn. I shone my torch into the void.

Eureka!

A narrow, murky, tunnel miraculously appeared; my prayers had been answered. I'd found it. Carter lives again!

Not exactly an Egyptian tomb, leaden with treasure but, nonetheless, a more-than acceptable ancient London tunnel appeared; maybe seven foot high and three foot wide and it stretched out like a giant rabbit's burrow in front of me. Buzzing with insects, damp from lack of air and smelling of a musty decay, it seemed to meander away into the distance. Naturally, I wanted to dive straight in and head for the unknown but a nagging voice in my head advised caution. Reluctantly, I instead rewound the string all the way back to the base of the ladder. As I again checked the time, ten twenty-five p.m., he appeared: the Earl. If he had been waiting for me, he never said, but welcomed me as one might a long lost, much valued colleague. Neither his tardiness nor my discovery were discussed.

A short while later, at his insistence, we arrived at the wooden door to his underworld apartment and proceeded inside. The whisky made a welcome reappearance and we toasted The Queen, the Commonwealth and Her Majesty's loyal subjects.

"May I start with an apology, Your Royal Highness, I may have mislead you when you were last here."

He gulped a large mouthful of the amber liquid as if bracing himself.

"So you lied to me?"

"Of course not, sir, I'm as incapable of lying as a, let me see, a US president or a minister for state in Her Majesty's government. No sir, rather the whole truth was not fully, completely and exhaustively presented in a manner more usually associated with candour and frankness.

"So you lied to me!"

"Absolutely not sir. Circumstances merely dictated that discretion needed to be applied to the delicate counterbalancing considerations which prevailed upon the various protagonists involved in the sensitive issues prevalent at that time."

"So you *did* lie to me."

" … Yes sir."

"Carry on then."

"Very well Your Highness. Strictly speaking, what we have here is not an officially recognised organisation."

"It's not?"

"No sir, MI5, palace division, was disbanded some years ago and the underground protection discontinued."

"I see… "

"Rodgers and I were in deep disagreement with the decision of the then PM but, it being just after the war, austerity and all that that entailed, plus the extreme unlikelihood of an underground attack, or so *they* considered, it was decided the operation should close."

"Rodgers?"

"A fine naval officer, sir, slightly before your time; saw action in the Far East. We decided, Rodgers and I, to take action, to secure the Royal Household and indeed, if I may be so bold, the very future of the royal family itself. Probably best if I do not explain the minutiae of how we achieved our objective; suffice to say that from nineteen fifty-two through to the present time both Rodgers and I with a little help from Jones, have had the privilege of protecting your good selves: that is until last April, when my colleague, still a young man of just sixty-five, passed away on active duty. This is why Jones and I decided to inform you, sir. With only two of us, the protection has somewhat weakened and of course, with there being no MI5 to report to, the situation has become... unsatisfactory."

"Quite."

"Your Highness, if there was any other way, we would not have involved you personally, but could we have trusted MI5 to do the right thing? The honourable thing? I think not!"

"Well, yes, naturally, you... had to act; to take action."

"Indeed we did sir. We decided that Jones should take the initial step: introduce you. If you remember, late at night, after one of your midnight walks, he showed you the sliding panel. He was very nervous. Still is rather, but it was the only way, you understand, the only way. To inform anybody else might... "

"Amazing, utterly amazing, Earl... all this time... underneath. But surely, nobody could... can attack the palace in this way."

"They can and they have sir."

The Earl rises and walks to a filing cabinet near the door. He pulls out two large leather-bound volumes; the first marked 'Interception Log' and the second, 'Research Log: Tunnelling Devices'. He flits from one to the other as if pulling together scattered thoughts. In the gloom, I can see that the logs contain not only hand-written and typed-up pages, but several well-thumbed copies of Stan Lee comic books. Curious indeed! Finally, he picks up the first log and flips to the last page.

"Two confirmed attempts, four probables and five possibles."

"Good gracious. Are you serious? Pass it over."

"I think it best if you do not see the contents sir. Relations with most of the countries involved are currently good and it could jeopardise Foreign Office and MI6 initiative if you had access, but may I assure you that all possible vigilance is being maintained. Jones does upstairs and I do downstairs. We have plans, sir, Jones and I to recruit at least one new member in the near future."

Crackpot. That's what I thought.

Unbelievable!

A vigilante, underworld surveillance team, if you could call it a team; self-appointed, unrewarded and unfinanced. Clearly this man's intentions, and indeed those of Jones and Rodgers, God rest his soul, were very public spirited; commendable, but to go to this extent, to live like moles, vermin, in unchartered, unhygienic conditions… preposterous! Nutters, all three of them! My instinct was to blast the whole thing clean out of the water, but something held me back. I deferred. This whole situation needed further consideration.

What if he was right: that enemies were constantly trying to get at us, we could be left vulnerable; open to attack. The PM had never even mentioned such an eventuality and he paid Her Majesty a visit practically every week. I'm sure Elizabeth would have taken me into her confidence, had he done so. Was it possible our self-appointed Earl of Buckingham, however unlikely as it may appear, might indeed be right? He had the proof, after all, in those large dossiers of his. Perhaps MI5 had never discussed the matter with the current PM. I considered an ever greater issue. If I was to blow his cover, MI5 would be all over the palace underground; faster than a rash over a bouncing baby's bottom, and my escape tunnel, the one I had spent so long looking for, and had only just located, would be sealed… forever.

I looked across. There he was, sat in his threadbare armchair, clearly very pleased with himself, the prospect of a knighthood, at some future point in time, written all over his smugly-contented face. He took out his pipe whilst leaving me to contemplate and offer both congratulation and suggestion as to the future. Finally, I broke my silence.

"You've done a marvellous job."

"Thank you, sir."

"I wish I could offer more support, particularly in the circumstances but, as I'm sure you are aware, that particular prospect is impossible for the foreseeable future, so I must decline to become in any way involved. Your selflessness and devotion to duty, commendable though they are, must remain invisible; your undoubted diligence and application, unrewarded. Our meetings have never taken place."

"But sir, if I may… "

"You may not sir," I interjected. "Consider your position and mine. The credibility of the royal family could be totally undermined. Secrecy is of the utmost!"

It was his turn to follow *my* lead.

We spoke no more of duty, but indulged in idle chit-chat. Family; his rarely seen except on the occasional bank holiday – they liked to go caving – and mine; growing up so quickly and with so little time to appreciate their early years. We discussed Christmas, Easter, Ascot and Epsom. Between us, we debated important issues; the state of the world, Warwickshire cricketing woes, wild life, will there be drought? Which do you prefer, The Beatles or The Kinks?

Time slipped by as we discussed the vagaries of the world.

I looked at my watch. One a.m. A ladder to climb.

"You must miss old Rodgers," I ventured, "dead and gone after a lifetime of devotion to Queen and country."

"Dead and gone, sir? He's most certainly dead, but I did not say he was gone… "

I was pleased to make my way out of the shaft and back to my quarters; away from the flies and the mud and the stench. One felt a pang of guilt for the Earl; poor misguided soul, guarding the palace, protecting the royals, with only a corpse for company.

16.

St James's Park Lake
sparkled under the moonlit sky

"The Mall. Can you picture it? You're one third the way down. Admiralty Arch is straight ahead. Behind you, the enormous great Queen Victoria monument, protecting the gates. You must see it now. That's where it is; exactly where you're standing: the exit; my escape route from the palace. There's a small cafeteria and a path that leads to that pretty little bridge over the lake. What's it called? Yes, yes… The Blue Bridge, I believe. Lots of squirrels running about; grey. No need to protect those! Are you with me?"

The therapist takes notes, eyes down, and Prince Philip continues.

One had no idea in the beginning, he remembers. Would have been so much better to be briefed by the Earl. He was the expert after all; knew his stuff; the ins and outs of life underground; the getting away. Couldn't be helped though, could it? Had to sally forth on my own, and so I did; not the first time may I say. Teenage years all over again.

My first foray into the unknown was on a midweek night in late October, or was it early November? In any case it was shortly after my second meeting with the Earl and not long after our boys had won the World Cup; the Germans: only time you know. After nightfall was the only practical time. Much safer and far easier to effect one's disguise. I had an old red wig, a leftover from a Hogmanay, and a pair of nice-quality sunglasses, a gift from one of those Caribbean big-wigs who came to visit, and an old swagman hat from my Australian navy days, minus the corks, of course. Wore a full length raincoat with lapels and all finished off with a pair of black rubber wellies. If I say so myself, I looked a sight. My own mother would have carried on by without a second glance. But that was the easy bit: the dressing up.

Down the ladder, I jumped off as usual and prepared to plunge a new marker in the mud pile. The new anchor was a horseshoe, partly for good luck and partly out of guilt. I know it's silly, but the sight of one's family up to their necks in the squelchy muck was beginning to make me feel distinctly queasy. It's impossible to explain fully but, somehow the gentle fun of submerging one's nearest and dearest in the stinking sludge had begun to lose its undoubted charm. In any case, my family snow globe had, I'd noticed, begun to tarnish: bits of it coming away. Swap for a horseshoe, I thought. Sensible.

As I began organising the string for the horseshoe, I

glanced at my watch and realised I was again running late. Should I waste valuable time relieving my family of their duty or leave it for some future excursion? I knew Her Majesty and indeed all of my family, had they known, would not have shirked from their duty and would expect nothing less of me. Anne, in particular, was never happier than when up to her eyes in it: the horse variety.

Easy decision really.

Decommission all of you on my return, my sludge-covered darlings, I promised, and I again shoved the lot of them in deep into the oozy, black mire; still waving, still happy and contented on their snow-covered balcony.

I unwound the string and crept past the Earl's sitting room door, taking care not to make a noise. Inside I could hear the muffled sound of a favourite television programme: *The Avengers* or *Coronation Street*, not sure which, though how his reception underground was so much better than mine above ground was a complete mystery. I rounded the corner, turned the knob on the tunnel door and shone the torch into the void. The hidden passage lit up; my very own Tutankhamun burial chamber, but with none of the Egyptian trimmings or even a token mummy. Wondered where the Earl kept old Rogers. Flies, I remember; lots of flies.

I took a deep breath. This is it!

I strode along, only slightly hunched. The tunnel was thankfully straightforward, in that, it was for the most part dry and clean, easy to navigate. The walls were solid: some sort of reinforced concrete, black with age and quite cold. Could have stored the wine. The ceiling, very similar; low, as I've said, nothing to spare. Better still, the tunnel did not diverge in different directions, but remained as a single passage, meandering, one hoped, its way to the great outdoors. I crossed a tiny trickle of a stream after approximately five minutes where the vibrations, of what I assume was traffic from above, were quite strong enough to be clearly felt. Otherwise, after just nine brisk minutes, my journey came to an end. A steep incline led up to a grey metal door. Livingstone could not have been happier. The hinges were on my left, but… darn it to hell, there was no handle on the right, just a keyhole, half way down.

Damn and blast, no blessed key. I checked everywhere: the ceiling, walls, the floor. Then I pushed the darn thing hard. Nothing. I looked for some sort of controlling number panel; becoming popular at the time, a coded push-button thingy. Again, nothing. Damn, damn, damn. I raised my fist to bash the door. Only just in time, I prevented myself, realising I had no idea what was the other side. Another deep breath; one must be patient. I turned to trudge back and stubbed my toe hard on a jutting-out rock. Holy Lord above! The pain was excruciating yet I could not yell; had to stifle it. Final straw! I grabbed the rock intending to fling as far as possible down the passage, but as I grabbed it, I noticed it came away far too easily. That's because it was actually a cover: a cleverly disguised lid, and underneath sat a hollowed out wooden box, maybe three inches square. Looking inside, one saw a key and a note. The note said, 'Do remember to put it back. Mr Rodgers!' The key went in the lock perfectly and I gently, quietly, turned the key to the left and pushed-open the door.

A white cubical appeared; small; no more than six square

feet, with a hand basin, coat rack and a toilet bowl. Cripes! I was in a lavatory: a toilet of all things! I closed the tunnel door, which was disguised on the toilet side to look like a plain tiled wall. It was finished off with a small mirrored cabinet. Ingenious, I thought. How very, very, clever.

Noise came flushing through, familiar noise. Toilet sounds; male, one assumed; men in various stages of relieving themselves; taps running and a dryer bursting in and out of life; coughing. I listened for a minute or two just to make sure. A public convenience without any doubt. I say; impressive, smart. Well done the Earl, and you too Mr Rodgers for your part; very well done both of you. Before I exited the cubicle door, which had layers of dust on an 'out of order' sign, I made use of the mirror on the cabinet. I took out my handkerchief and wiped the sunglasses, took out my comb, removed the wig and straightened my hair. I hand-dusted the raincoat and stood up straight, checking myself in the mirror. Wig replaced, glasses cleaned, lapels smoothed-down, the moment of truth beckoned; my public awaited. I opened the door and walked briskly out.

A man looked at me then quickly looked away, then another and another. Typically British, I thought, all ignoring me; too busy, possibly too frightened to bother with a weirdo in some sort of fancy dress. I washed my hands so as not to look conspicuous, checked one last time and walked out.

The night was warm for the time of year and a wonderful sweet smell of freedom hung in the air. On the right was the ladies' toilets, and around the corner, a coffee shop, just about to close for the night. On the pretty bridge to the right, the world had gathered, despite the lateness of the hour:

sweethearts; young and old; families with children and owners with dogs, all out much too late. St James's Lake sparkled under the moonlit sky. One wished Elizabeth were here, my darling Elizabeth. I turned left, up a small incline to Marlborough Gate and then onto a wide thoroughfare: The Mall. Eyes left, Queen Victoria and Buckingham Palace. Eyes right, Admiralty Arch and freedom.

As I stepped out on the footpath, I noticed a leaflet on the ground, a flyer, you might say, promoting our great capital. 'London is yours' it read. 'See it today'. But before I could pick it up, a carefree wind whisked it away, all the way down the tree-lined boulevard towards The Arch. I turned for a moment looking down at the palace. A wave of regret came over me. I felt like a traitor, thoroughly ashamed, but I consoled myself with the knowledge that I simply had to carry on. My very sanity depended on it.

I turned my back on the palace and followed that carefree flyer all the down The Mall. 'London is yours', it said. 'See it today'.

17

What if The Queen is looking out the window?

I wandered back via Green Park, just one of several thousand visitors.

It seemed strange that nobody rushed up to greet me, shake one's hand and offer refreshment, nor was there, from any of the benches or railings, the smell of fresh paint that normally accompanied a royal visit. Once or twice, someone crossed my path, clearly in breach of protocol, but I resisted pointing out the error of their ways. A navy officer with his wife approached, Canadian I believe. He pointed out Buckingham Palace, my palace, and I instinctively smiled and held out my hand before realising, almost too late.

Green Park: wonderfully functional, don't you think, with its army of trees in neat columns and its walkways and benches to rest aching legs. I sat down, observed the passing world, and straightened my wig.

A dishevelled gentleman approached.

He was carrying a large tattered bag and was even worse dressed than I: a feat of no little accomplishment. He tottered from side to side, a result, no doubt, of the near-empty whisky bottle in his left hand and what looked like a pronounced limp. He glared in my direction.

"Get off."

"You get off," I replied.

"I was here first."

"Now look here, sir, I'll not stand for this. A man has an absolute right to sit on whatever park bench he wishes, provided it's available. This one is and I shall."

"A toff?"

"What's it to you? And do you know who you're addressing, sir?"

"You're on my bench. I sleep here, now get off!" he retorted.

"Shan't."

"I'll have to chuck you off then… toff!"

"Shall you indeed?" I replied. "Come on, come on, if you dare."

He swung at me like a girl, left and right; no coordination; all effort, no precision; truly atrocious timing. A combination of odours followed each attempted punch. Stinking breath, fresh whisky and a whiff of the seriously unwashed accompanied each revolving lunge. One could so easily have taken advantage, but somehow I could not. I allowed him to flap and flail until he finally gave up, placing two untested fists on two very weary knees; head down, panting hard. Just as well I resisted. When I turned around a policeman, a copper on the beat, stood there eying both of us as he casually fingered his truncheon.

"And what seems to be the matter gentlemen?"

"Nothing officer, nothing at all," I replied.

My would-be assailant, not so drunk as to worsen an already precarious situation, agreed.

"This toff was trying to nick my seat, officer. I always sleep here, it's my bench, but… I suppose, well… it might be OK to share… for a while."

"You two should be ashamed of yourselves. What if The Queen is looking out the window?"

"She's always in bed by nine-thirty."

My words were out before my brain engaged.

"Oh… and you're an authority on Her Majesty's sleeping arrangements, are you *sir*?"

There was note of derision in the policeman's voice which bordered on insolence.

"Of course," I replied, "it's common knowledge Her Majesty retires early midweek… "

"And no doubt, you also know what she has for her breakfast, *sir*?" he smirked.

"As it happens I do," I replied helpfully, "everyone knows."

He looked genuinely interested, one eyebrow raised, so I carried on.

"Actually, she likes a scrambled egg, soft, with some toast and marmalade and… "

"Enough! I'll have both of you flung in the cells till you sober up."

"Sorry officer. We shall behave, shan't we?"

"Yes, constable, yes." And my 'colleague' nodded in agreement.

The bench was shared. He took the far-end three quarters, stretched out and made a pillow of his tatty bag. But I had the better view of the palace and more than enough space. He stank. Not as badly as the palace underground but, heavens above, far worse than one's woollen socks after a day at the stables.

I looked over towards Elizabeth's window on the north wing. It was dark: lights out, silent and still. Only to be expected. It was ten-thirty, after all. A second wave of embarrassment and regret rushed over me. Little did she know how I was cheating on her, taking a large slice of freedom without her permission. I wanted to confess, to rush back and beg forgiveness. I felt dirty, unclean like a man who had purposely chosen to cheat on his perfect, loving, generous wife. Freedom, even my scant, limited version came with a price-tag.

The night cooled quickly, and as the park emptied, I also decided I should return home.

My drunken friend stirred and grunted on the bench. He half sat up and rubbed his eyes.

"Navy?"

"How did you know?"

"You're a toffee-nosed git, that's how."

"I warn you sir, I'm not above… " and I looked to see where the policeman was.

"Oh shut it toff. How long you been out?"

"… Fourteen years in a month or so."

"Sorry for your troubles, mate; can't be easy coming down in the world."

"I'm not down in the world, not at all... one is simply... "

"Yeah, yeah, neither am I toff, neither am I... ex-navy myself, guvnor."

"You are? What ship?"

"The *Valiant*. You heard of her? The finest battleship... saw action, you know; finest vessel... ever to sail the seas... "

With that, the whisky again overtook and he dozed off.

Memories flood back.

The *Valiant*; marvellous ship; I can see her now; the power; the might; the majesty. The *Valiant* of my mind's eye sails out through the palace gates, transverses a miraged Queen Victoria Memorial and ghosts down The Mall; twenty knots, steady as she goes; out under Admiralty Arch, across Trafalgar Square and into the London night; serene, silent and wonderful. My ex-navy colleague, reeking of body odour and booze, snores and whistles all the while, a steady, respectful rhythm as if in salute of the magnificent sight. Finally, the ship evaporates from view.

No sooner had she disappeared, than the whisky bottle rolled from the poor man's hand. One felt a pang of sympathy for the old seafarer. By the state of him, it appeared he was well used to sleeping rough. His coat was worn and torn, his trousers held up with a piece of chord. He wore no socks and both his boots had holes in them. It was hard to imagine this level of deprivation outside the gates of one's own palace. Nevertheless, there he was, and ex-navy to boot. I decided there and then to do something for him. In my left hand pocket I found a ten shilling note. I took off my wellingtons. I took off my socks. By now, he was soundly asleep and when

I eventually sneaked away, he never knew a thing, but I'm sure he was grateful when he woke the next morning to find the socks I left him. As for me, I bought a new pair, shortly afterwards, with the ten shillings I'd found in my pocket.

I glanced one last time towards Her Majesty's bedroom and was surprised to see her bedroom light come on, then the light in my study and finally, a dim light in my bedroom. Not more than twenty seconds later, all three lights went out again, in reverse order. Dashed home bloody quickly, I can tell you!

That first night of adventure was rapidly followed by several more. I became brave, some might say foolhardy. I started chatting to the locals, the tourists, everybody. I wanted to find out what the public really thought of we royals; or to put it simply, were we royals really real or were we royals not really as real as real royals ought to be?

I was amazed at what I heard.

People are very free with their tongues, let me tell you and so gullible. For example, they actually believe what they read. If the newspapers say one's marriage is on the rocks, they believe it! Incredible. Even at the height of my darkest period, I never considered a separation, nor Elizabeth... I'm sure. Marriage is a duty and a privilege. Royal marriages are amazingly solid and always will be... most of them.

One night, I sat down for a late evening coffee when two Japanese tourists ambled by. We exchanged small talk as one does and then I asked.

"Do you like the royals?"

"Queen, like. Him very grumpy."

I almost flew into a rage. Grumpy? Me grumpy? Stupid, ridiculous... maddening!

"Him not grumpy at all," I said, "him… misunderstood."

The taller one looks me up and down, clearly appreciating my co-ordinated attire.

"You know royal persons?" she replies, with half a grin.

"How I know?" I responded. "But him not grumpy. Him happy, him very nice."

"Look at paper here," the smaller says and she hands it over.

On the front page of one of those damned red tops, was a picture of a beaming Queen and slightly serious me; well perhaps more than slightly. It had been taken at Badminton, several months previously, and a horse, Anne's, if I'm not mistaken, had just stood on my foot. The caption underneath stated in huge, impossible to miss, lettering: 'Glorious Queen, grumpy Philip!'

"Him not angry, him in pain," I explained, through gritted teeth.

"How you know? You not there."

"I there… I there in crowd," I responded.

They went away giggling, but strangely, not at all convinced.

I hate the press. They can call me whatever they want, damn them to hell. Always putting me down. I'm not grumpy. I'm never grumpy, and my celebrated wit; unique, even if I say so myself. They never find space to comment on that, I notice. Oh no: my much admired wit!

With the children away at school, The Queen and The Queen Mother frequently away and with my duties often finished early, I found I could get away, almost at will. Terrific. Find some old tat, the older the better, clobber it on and off I went.

At first, I stayed close to home: Charing Cross, Leicester Square, and the like. Then I started catching late-evening buses and tubes. People would look at me in disbelief. I could see the distain in their eyes: this old, unkempt, bedraggled ruffian in wellingtons, with tousled red hair and dark glasses, wandering across their idyllic evening... spoiling it. One or two, thinking I was about to beg, had their purses at the ready; drop a coin and dash away. Can't say I blamed them, I really did look a sight. Occasionally a tramp looked for funds from me. Vindication from one's peers, one might say, but very off-putting. Mostly, however, the experience of being free of the royal shackles was excellent; superb. Loved it; loved it, I tell you. I was born to be free.

Another evening, late November I believe; chilly, the occasional snow flurry, enough to make one's blood turn blue, I wandered into a tourist shop. You know the kind: bunting in the window, Union Jack tea-towels and Union Jack shorts; royal plates, cups, silverware; taxis, buses, Big Bens and Little Venices, all in various sizes; ash trays and post boxes. I was enjoying wandering around, though I could feel the eyes of the shop manageress eyeing my every move. Not her normal customer, one felt sure! As it happened, I needed a new mug for the office back at the palace, so I decided to look for something nice in porcelain, with just the two of us on, equals. If they did a matching pair at the right price, who knows, I may have treated Her Majesty to a surprise. Over to the cup and plate shelf, I began my search. Well, one was most disappointed. Wall to wall queens, both mum and daughter and others besides; Annes, Charles', Andrews and Edwards by the truck load; corgis and dorgis, beefeaters, palaces and castles, all on cups, mugs and plates. But where was I? Nowhere! I checked everywhere. The bloody disappearing prince, that's what I was, the forgotten Johnny bloody Foreigner; the invisible consort. Needless to say I called the manageress over, by now so furious I completely forgot I was in disguise. Teeth clenched, arms flailing, I spelt it out.

"I've looked everywhere. I should be here, don't you think? Everyone else is. All I need is a blasted mug, for heaven's sake. Look … look! Can *you* see me? It's not fair. We should all be here, all of us, don't you think? Can *you* tell me where I am?"

Her eyes, suspicious when she arrived, became confused and then sympathetic. She placed a gentle hand on my shoulder.

"Don't know where you are, sir? Are you lost? Don't know your way? I do understand, sir, truly. All you need is a mug, a warming mug of something wholesome on a chilly winter's evening."

She took my hand and led me outdoors.

"There's a very friendly soup kitchen just down the road, and I'm sure they would love to look after you, sir; maybe even find you a nice warm bed for the night."

18

The grinding tedium became the grinding tolerable

From bathroom to Mall, eighteen minutes flat. How about that!

I was becoming a regular Billy Whizz underground. Escape to the great outdoors became almost routine. Obviously one had to be careful. It would have been easy to become blasé; reckless. Getting back home was frequently problematic. One sometimes had to wait until the appropriate moment to go through the 'out of order' toilet door and into the cubicle, but if I'm honest, it was all getting very easy; a little too easy, in fact. What's the point in defeating the system, if there's nobody to share the victory with? Strangely, I wished Elizabeth could join in and Margaret, just like the old days. In another life the princesses, as they were, would have loved all of this: the excitement: the deception: the great escape down The Mall.

Jones knew of course. The pained look on his face said it all; his penchant for a furtive sideways glance with accompanying heavy sigh, a dead giveaway. The Earl also knew, I was sure. I shuffled past his subterranean living quarters on my errands out, making no particular effort to conceal my movements. But could I discuss my gallivanting with either of them? Relate the evening adventures? Of course not. Had some of my ex-navy pals been around, or better still, complicit in my escapades, it would have been so much more fun. But contact could not be made; impossible. They had their own lives to lead. One needed to count one's blessings and one did.

My early-morning darkness had lifted immeasurably and I suddenly felt very lucky with my lot; decidedly happier, I have to say; more at peace. Public engagements were far less fraught and less of a monumental chore. The grinding tedium became the grinding tolerable. Imagine being able to say 'well done' to some dreadful windbag, who had stood and delivered a long, drivelling, instantly forgettable speech. I could and I did... frequently. My own speeches, had, in contrast, improved substantially. Everyone said so. Elizabeth smiled at me more often, and straightened my tie less often. My moods were immeasurably better and those blackened mountains, ever-threatening to overwhelm me, lacked their former power. But they were by no means defeated. Absolutely not! More needed to be achieved. Much more.

I wondered what the Earl thought. Was he still planning to expand his underground surveillance; to find a replacement for Rodgers? Had he found help? Another mole? Was he about to concede defeat, and turn himself in to MI5? I dared not ask. The less we knew about each other the better. But, as it happened, it didn't take much longer to find out.

I came home one Wednesday night in early December and stepped, as usual, through the secret toilet door. I shone my torch down the tunnel. My heart jumped and I nearly dropped the damn thing. The Earl had been waiting in the dark like some overbearing parent waiting for junior to arrive home from the disco.

"Blasted fool; you scared the life out of me."

"We have to talk, Your Highness."

"We do? Where?"

"My sitting room, sir."

He led and I followed, regaining my composure. The room was more or less the same as before. Royal adulation covered the walls and a whisky soon appeared, but his air had changed. Gone was the assuredness of a man who knew his purpose; who knew his efforts would ultimately be rewarded and whose sacrifice, in this, his self-imposed quarantine, would ultimately be recognised and rewarded. Instead of the shrewd, confident officer of just two months previous, a pale imitation served the drinks and grappled for reassurance, for confirmation and, more importantly, for some way forward. I allowed him to do the talking. He clearly needed to.

He scolded me.

"I would not presume to, in any sense, advise you sir," he advised, "but surely you must see how dangerous your actions are."

"Well, hardly 'dangerous'."

"You could be kidnapped, sir, or assaulted, or get run-over by a vehicle. Jones is of the same opinion. I feel so responsible. I should never have allowed you near the tunnel and now, obviously having tasted the freedom… "

"It's not your fault. I would have found it eventually, and the key. "

"Please sir, consider your position. Consider The Queen and your family. If anything should happen…"

"No one would dare attempt capture," I countered. "Not me nor any member of the family. Abroad perhaps but, rest assured, not here in London."

He was on his third whisky by the time I had had one, and a wall of cigarette smoke enveloped him. Forgot to offer me one, I noticed! Clearly, he needed a decent night's sleep to boot, but more than that, he needed peace of mind.

I changed subject.

"You look like you're not eating properly. There's a banquet tomorrow night; the frogs, I think. Would you like me to drop off some leftover quiche and crudités? Maybe other odds and ends and a nice bottle of red?

"Thank you sir, you're very kind."

"Think nothing of it. I'll lower a tuck bag down the shaft when everyone has gone."

"Awfully good of you, sir."

My offer of food and a top-class rouge did nothing to lift his spirits. He sat there glumly, slinging back drink after drink, by now invisible within his own grey cloud. I began to worry and not just for him. He was keeper of my freedom, was he not? If he should do something daft, the game could so easily be up. I felt I needed to come up with something.

"My good man, how about you tag along, some evening?"

"Tag along, sir?"

"Yes; see I don't get into trouble."

"No, sir, really I… "

"You'll see what I do and be reassured that I'm not doing anything dangerous. Besides, you need some fresh air. Awfully stuffy down here. I insist."

"It's not appropriate, sir. We haven't been formally… "

"It's an order, not a request," I responded. "I'll let you know. Be ready. I dare say we may have to move quickly."

I do love a little deference, don't you? In fact I love a lot of deference, but one must be careful and never abuse one's position of power. Golden rule! Nor should you use a proverbial sledgehammer to crack a proverbial nut. A medium sized hammer will normally do. I knew it would be good for him, tagging along. He didn't even have to dress up!

The opportunity arrived sooner than expected: within a few days, as it happened, not long before Christmas. Needless to say, our first expedition was more than a little tentative. He instantly adopted the role of bodyguard, trying to be everywhere at once: out front, at my side, then out the back. I was anxious to try one of those new-fangled pizzas up Wardour Street, while he was constantly looking out for would-be assailants. He looked spruce in a lounge suit accompanying me, a red-haired tramp in wellies. What a combination! As the evening wore on, he relaxed somewhat and became less of a stuffed shirt. It transpired he was quite an aficionado on the architecture and history of London.

"Admiralty Arch," I proffered.

"Designed by Webb, built by Mowlem and completed just before the Great War, sir."

"St James's Palace."

"Commissioned by Henry the Eighth. Pre-eminent until Queen Victoria's time. Rich history, some of it quite bloody."

And so it went; history on the hoof.

At the end of the evening, the Earl was out on his feet. But it had done him good. Clearly needed the exercise. Would have made an excellent tour guide, my underworld pal, had he not opted for protecting royal tramps and decomposing bodies. I was very pleased with myself. A fillip for the Earl and, surprisingly, a much-appreciated sight-seeing friend for me. We agreed, at my suggestion, he would accompany me more or less once a month as an informal bodyguard-companion.

Pleasing, I had to say; yes, very, very pleasing indeed, and a load off my mind to boot. I would, from then on, be able to keep tabs on my underground companion; ensure he didn't do anything hasty. But the Earl, as I was about to find out, had plenty on his mind too.

19

Can we find coffins for them, and disinfectant?

Prince Philip re-joins the present, turns away from the window, and eyes his therapist with suspicion. She sits in the corner, diligently tapping at her keyboard. He wonders why she writes so much and says so little.

"This won't get out will it? Our sessions; you have to promise. Go ahead, as I've said. Take notes if you must; no skin off my nose."

He paces up and down.

"Now where was I? Late sixty-six. I think. Shall I carry on? Yes, winter sixty-six; early December, unless I'm mistaken; shortly before Sandringham."

You see, now that I had the services of the Earl, I could start planning daytime expeditions. Riskier of course, but equally, a great deal more exciting. The city: so much more interesting in daylight, don't you think? Parks for example. Much more pleasurable enjoying Regent's Park in its full glory by light of day; no question. Or a pretty young thing skipping down Kings Road in one of those delightful miniskirts, eh? Or taking-in Nelson's Column with its legion of pigeons. So friendly, the London pigeon, I always think; will feed straight from the hand, you know. Far better in daylight, I think you'll agree; yes? I wondered, at one point, if Elizabeth would allow me a small coup... a hundred or so, no more; unobtrusive. Down the bottom end; plenty of space.

As we strolled along The Embankment, the Earl and I, he dropped the first bombshell.

"I must confess, sir; there's more than one."

"One what?"

"Body, sir."

"Not just Rodgers?"

"No sir, Wilson and Walters."

"Boxed?"

"No sir."

"Thought as much; the whiff is quite something. Look, one can see St Paul's from here. – In the line of duty?"

"Yes sir, nineteen sixty-two and nineteen sixty-four, respectively. The southern aspect is the most interesting, in my opinion."

"I prefer the western. Wonderful symmetry. Amazing it survived the blitz. You've kept them together... the bodies?"

"Truly amazing, sir: unquestionably a work of genius. Wren was very, very accomplished sir, and yes they are. I have them stacked quite close to the brick wall at the far end, near

The *Evening Standard*s. No ventilation, unfortunately, but I do occasionally open the tunnel doors. It's a public toilet so it's only to be expected, sir."

"The pong, you mean?"

"Yes, sir."

"Slightly different odours don't you think? Is that the Tower Bridge to our right?"

"So it is, sir; what a wonderful construction and yes, I agree they are different but I only ever hold the outside door open for a maximum of fifteen minutes. One does not wish to attract the attention of the police or vermin."

"Sensible."

"Thank you sir."

Needless to say, one was a tad concerned. There were all sorts of implications. If the bodies were discovered, would I be implicated, or even The Queen? One decomposing body underneath one's palace is regrettable, two, downright careless, but the discovery of three would be an absolute scandal. And what of the deceased themselves? Were they the right sort of chaps to be populating one's underground? Public school, one hoped, career in the civil service or forces, and that alone would probably be enough to get The Queen and I off the hook, but if any were of, say, questionable background, like a banker for example, there could be all hell to pay. The public, quite correctly, would expect one's deceased population to be predominately public school: private, as opposed to the equally possible, public school: public; clarity was needed, I think you'll agree. Rodgers was fine; ex-navy, but, as yet, I knew nothing of the other two.

The extra bodies also threw more light on the Earl himself, so to speak.

As a monarch, one is not used to being lied to and if there's lying to be done, there exists an established protocol, unwritten, of course. One should never have the remotest inkling that a lie has been perpetrated. All lies need to be seamless, plausible and as casual as possible. For example:

'Investitures all day today dear; wonderful'.
'Thank you madam chairperson, for that rather lengthy introduction'.
'Yes darling, fudge is, I'm sure, enriched with vitamins'.

You see… easy, but the Earl admitted his lie; shocking! And by doing so, I now became an accomplice to the act or acts! That sort of thing may be all very well and fine for prime ministers, other members of parliament, and for rank and file public officials but we royals have to be above such moral failings. As Her Majesty's subjects know, royals are incapable of telling, or being complicit in a lie, though occasional misunderstandings, as I said earlier, are allowable. Therefore, knowledge of just one illicit, decomposing body, if found, is a permissible lapse of judgement but two, or, as in this case three, and all at different times and presumably from different causes, calls into question the integrity of the entire monarchy. Our very existence could be threatened and, even worse, The Queen, if she found out, would be very annoyed indeed.

"Can we find coffins for them and disinfectant?"

"Well of course, sir, I did consider using coffins, but the practicality of purchasing without suspicion, delivering to the public toilets, then manoeuvring them down the narrow tunnel and on my own… well, sir… nigh on impossible.

Then there's the hoisting of the decomposed deceased, single-handedly, into the coffins and… "

"Yes, quite; one gets the picture," I replied. "Obviously you should have had a corpse management facility installed while you still had some help; silly boy."

The Earl carried on.

"But I like the disinfectant idea; yes indeed sir; shall definitely look into your suggestion. Have we time to take in The Tate?"

My underground friend had become an enigma. On the one hand, he displayed an excellent knowledge of the capital, and his taste in home-decoration, and on limited means judging by his sitting-room, was beyond reproach, but his handling of some straight-forward cadavers left something to be desired. Any idiot should have known that if one was to keep a collection of the deceased close to one's living quarters, and the normal boxing-up could not be effected, then the liberal use of disinfectant would be an absolute necessity. It's not as if the costs would have been prohibitive. Upstairs, we purchased our disinfectant in bulk, from the wholesalers, and it worked out very reasonable indeed.

The second bombshell was equally unnerving.

"Underground attacks," I enquired. "That dossier you have, and not, of course, wishing to invade the private nature of your activities… "

"Ah, I meant to speak to you about that, sir."

"What do you mean?"

"I'm sorry, sir, but… there haven't been any. I wish I could say there had; that many people had been killed, mutilated, disfigured and suffered terribly; that we had saved several members of the royal family, including yourself, of course, corgis and children… but alas, I cannot."

"The dossier… I saw it myself… in your hands."

"Fabrication sir… lies. MI5 also wanted proof but we had none. That's the real reason they closed us down. But simply because it never happened, is no indication the palace is safe from malevolent attack. You have to understand, sir. Have you seen the episode in *The Avengers* comic where 'The Mole' attacks New York, from under the subway? It's shocking sir. If the Russians or aliens from outer space got hold of one of those things and unleashed it under the palace, well, who knows the havoc it could wreak? We are the first line of defence, or rather I am, Your Highness. But I am most dreadfully sorry I misled you and I promise, there will be no more surprises; no new corpses; just Rodgers, Wilson and Walters… and Smith. "

He could see I was unmoved by his explanation and in truth, a broken man stood in front of me.

"I understand," I replied. "Sometimes things… can't be helped."

Neither of us knew what to say next, both of us locked in awkward silence, but as luck would have it, the opportunity to 'mend fences', as it were, arrived sooner than either of us expected.

20

She chose well, did The Queen; yes; very, very well indeed

Just a few days had passed when I knocked on his door, hoping to lift his spirits… and mine!

Her Majesty had been unavoidably delayed on a trip to open a chocolate fudge factory; complained of bellyache, of all things and had to have a lie down. As it was a magnificent and unseasonably warm winter's afternoon, I simply itched for a few overs at the crease. Who better for a knock than my underground acquaintance, the Earl. He'd never mentioned, but I felt sure he was a cricketer. One can tell!

All padded up, bewigged and bespectacled, I galloped down the ladder and rapped on his door. Naturally he was delighted to see me after such a brief interval and we wandered over to the park: Green Park, like a pair of overgrown school kids, never once mentioning bodies, smells, coffins or disinfectant.

The park was thronged with tourists but, as luck would have it, we found enough space near Canada Gate and set up stumps. Amazing for December, the crease was quite firm, but then there had been little rain and it was rather mild. I won the toss and chose to bat. Like moths to a light, a large crowd gathered round to cheer us on, several volunteering for field duties. Superb!

We were half-a-dozen overs into our game (twenty-two for no wicket, I believe), when the most unbelievable thing happened. One simply could not make it up.

We took a short break on one of the benches near the park gates, to ease our aching limbs. Out of the blue, Brian Johnson and Denis Compton wandering home, one presumes from BBC commitments, happened upon our match and instantly, upon recognising the quality of the participants, took up commentary positions. I decided there and then to abandon my disguise and show the assembled crowd what a real consort could do! Our two commentators climbed a nearby tree, near the park gates, and sat on a low bough; palace behind. Their perch was ideal to see over the heads of the spectators and away into the distance, taking-in, not only the entire Green Park, but a sizeable chunk of St James's to boot!

Johnson sets the scene.

'Buckingham from the St James's End… long loping stride… that's a wide.'

'First time at Green Park, Denis?'

'Yes Jonners, wonderful grounds though; ideal winter venue... dry wicket; should suit the batter, I'll wager.'

'Buckingham again... this time with a more purposeful run-up... and Windsor whacks it away... Oh what a stroke: wonderful, marvellous, impeccable timing. My word Denis, how about that?'

'The crowd love it, Jonners, loud applause, straight down the middle... Oh, I see it's almost time for tea. What's that you have there? Some leftover cake?'

'I'm too excited to eat... here he comes again, the Earl... Oh crikey, the prince has done it again, only this time it's gone for miles... All the way over The Mall and into St James's Lake... has to be a six, Denis, surely.'

'What a shot, Jonners. Let me tell you, there's a very surprised duck out in the middle of that lake; tremendous... Oh dear, sorry old bean, crumbs everywhere, it's a Victoria sponge.'

'Seriously, Denis, have you ever seen a finer opening bat. I'll say The Queen chose well when she chose that young Mountbatten for a consort. No finer Greek cricketer in all of England.'

'So you think it was a factor?'

'You mean his prowess with a bat, Denis?'

'Precisely.'

'Undoubtedly.'

'And what a delightful afternoon for such a prestigious event: the crowd love him, the young foreign import; applauding with aplomb, Jonners. Yes indeed, in these parts they know an up-and-coming sovereign when they see one... I'll say, Jonners, this cake is delicious.'

When I opened my eyes, I found I was seated alongside the Earl on a park bench. Must have nodded off for a minute or two, and the dream: so vivid! Shame I woke up; had my eye

117

in; could have made a century. The Earl had kept a look-out, while I dozed.

I looked at my seat; same one where I had had the pleasure of meeting my ex-navy colleague a few months prior. Wondered if he appreciated my gift, poor old beggar… the socks, if you remember.

We played a few more overs, the Earl and I, while the sun slid quietly beneath the horizon. Like the old days, I sprinted between wickets, getting up and down like a young roebuck. Never gave an inch. It got dark quickly, too quickly, but then it was winter. Was I happy? My brow dripped wet, despite rapidly cooling conditions; my wellies stank and I began to ache, but I was unencumbered and shackle-free, breathing-in God's own unrestricted air. I could so easily have swopped my privileged position for all of this; for freedom. Some day, I promised myself; some day and soon; something will have to give.

We played until we could see no more; the park shrouded in darkness. Nothing else for it; we upped wicket, shook hands and went home.

21

Stuffed bloody stiffs in their starched bloody shirts

Weeks and months pass. Daytime escapes, wonderful. Could have done with more! And family life at the palace; stimulating, invigorating. Children growing up fast, as they do; different ages, always something new going on. Charles off to Australia, Anne and her gymkhanas. Elizabeth – where to start? Manic with the public and private duties, dinners, lunches, investitures, so on and so forth. My duties you ask? How did I cope? Well, one has to be honest. I was as earnest and endeavouring as I could possibly muster. You see, my wife, she was made to be a queen; born to it; everybody said so. Conscientious beyond words, dedicated beyond belief and carrying the responsibility with a… how should one put it…? A consummate graciousness very few possess; very proud of her. Obviously I could never actually tell her, you understand. I'm only telling you because, well, you know why. As for me, simply not made of the same stuff. Ran away; had to; every opportunity; away. Scamper down that tunnel; escape. Fast, let me tell you; speed improving all the time. Bathroom to Birdcage Walk, twenty minutes. Beat that!"

Wigs. Needed new ones, better ones, longer ones and shorter; curly; in various colours; even toyed with a toupee. One or two cravats, ties for variety. Played it safe. Called Jones aside. Handed over a twenty and left it to him. As for my coats, Camden Market; that's the place. Ideal. Go into any clothes shop along the high street and the dafter your appearance, the better they liked you. I came home one chilly March afternoon with three top-quality gents' coats for less than a fiver! Full length too; a black, a grey and a not-at-all sure; yellow perhaps. Dark glasses: sale in Debenhams, so I picked up a black and a cream with a fancy gold trim. Bought a nice pair of Doc Martins, marked down, I remember; hats and trousers in Selfridges; such good value. And one or two trilbies, berets and a deer-stalker from a second-hand shop, quality items, but not expensive. They didn't all fit. Jackets and blazers: already had plenty at home, gathering dust.

Tried a false moustache, on one occasion. Decided against. Made me look rather silly… like Poirot!

Shoved everything under the bed. Had to be careful not to mix-up my excursion attire with the state gifts, though it must be said that many of those gifts were also gathering dust. Needed to find space somewhere else. Let's face it, the palace was bloody big enough, why did I have to shove them under my bed? Bad habit, I suppose. No space on the sitting room shelf, you see. Polynesian masks, French silver, South American gold trinkets, boxed and unboxed, large and small and nowhere to go. Thought of dropping off some stuff to the Earl, below. He still had some space in his display cabinet and, technically it was still Buckingham Palace, but in the end I decided against it; might have caused a diplomatic incident, were it ever to be found out.

Quite enjoyed dressing up, too. Mix and match. Mauve wig, black glasses, long yellow coat; blond wig, cream glasses, grey raincoat, shoes or wellies; all sorts really! This was the first time I realised how important it was for Her Majesty to match a two-piece with a hat and bag. Indeed, she was pleasantly surprised at my burgeoning interest in fashion etiquette. Rarely commented, of course, but the whimsical look on her face told me how much she appreciated my opinion on the suitability of her attire, and the colour combination she had chosen. I was surprised how easy it was to throw an ensemble together for my own private forays. Had a full length mirror screwed on my bathroom door for that precise purpose. Useful indeed.

Underground, things were also improving. The introduction of disinfectant had an immediate effect. The original four-body decomposing stench was now down to no more than, one would suggest, one and a half. The disinfectants the Earl had chosen were, in my opinion, inspired. On a Monday, he clearly used the pine and lavender; by Wednesday, he had switched to wild-ocean deep-clean and on the weekends his preference was for the evening-scented primrose petal or mid-summer syrup of strawberry. All most satisfying and there were fewer winged insects, I noticed.

One craved entertainment; always enjoyed singing, dancing, tomfoolery of any description, but my favourite undoubtedly was a good musical. The afternoon matinees around Leicester Square offered endless variety, and last minute, as one often was due to circumstances, excellent value was to be had for all the shows. The Earl also enjoyed these outings but I noticed he was frequently on edge while we stood in the queue. One never had to worry, while he was there. He kept an unobtrusive firearm in his jacket, sawn-off, and in the event of an attempted murder, kidnap or such like, one fully expected he would have been able to take-down a would-be assailant and guide me away in next to no time. His reaction speed was superb, as I discovered one Thursday afternoon.

We stood waiting for the excellent *Hello Dolly*, part of lengthy queue. A child's balloon burst. Without a moment's hesitation, the Earl sprang into action like a starved leopard in a chicken coup. Several more balloons popped before we realised there was no danger. Could have been nasty, though. Had to buy lots of ice cream, I can tell you. The Earl, I must say, was very efficient in sorting out the child's smallish flesh wound. Afterwards, he reloaded, just in case, then made full use of a wide range of first-aid materials from a concealed bag, kept hidden for just such occasions. The child's mother, one recalls, overreacted as mothers sometimes do, shouting, 'Call the police, he has a gun,' etc. etc. I had to inform her that the police only attend *serious* crime incidents; i.e., death, maiming and so forth, but not easy-to-fix children's flesh wounds. I paid for her tickets, and her ice cream, and that was that. Small price to pay, I think you'll agree. I have to say nothing really serious ever happened, beyond paying full price, one wet Wednesday, and we both enjoyed our theatre trips immensely.

Meanwhile, back at the palace, my own balloon popped.

My wife glared at me.

"Philip. You're slacking."

"No I'm not dear. Been doing my share."

"You've been skiving off every free afternoon. Don't deny it."

"Only cancellations and under bookings, my dear… and fog."

"But you used to do extra, Philip; make yourself useful, but these days it's off to the study or the library or even spending hours in the bathroom, of all places… with the tap running! Not good enough dear. We have to be seen to be interested, Philip; engaged."

"Perhaps I could do The Queen's Speech this year."

"Not amusing Philip. If they ever call it The Consort's Speech, you can do it."

"Yes darling."

"What charities have you?"

"Let me see; Animals, Wild Life, The Commonwealth, The Forces, Other War and Business Development."

"Don't exaggerate, Philip. 'Animals' falls under 'Wild Life'."

"Sorry darling."

"Now what else can one give you? Let me see… yes. Have Health, and you can also have Safety, that's a good one, what with all those life-saving chaps, swimming pools , beaches and Australians."

"That's not fair. Can't Anne pick up one or two? What about Charles or Margaret?"

"Anne only does horses and Scotland, as you well know and Charles will have his hands full soon enough trying becoming Welsh. And he has to learn to grow leeks this year."

"Drawn the short straw there," I agreed.

"As for my sister, she's more suited to foreign engagements; small tropical islands and the like."

"Yes, dear."

"That's right, Philip, and don't 'yes dear' me. You know it's for your own good."

"No dear, one would never 'yes dear' you dear."

I thought it through thoroughly.

More difficult, I surmised; practically impossible. More ribbon snipping, more hands to shake. Damn it to hell, how was I going to get out of this one? I tried to look on the bright side. I was beginning to tire somewhat, of being the single tramp about town. I had no one to play with, except the Earl occasionally, and he wasn't exactly a barrel of laughs. All very well fooling around on the South Bank or having the Japs take one's photo with the pigeons but truthfully my escapades had become less exciting than before, so perhaps these new duties were a blessing in disguise. Wrong, let me tell you, very, very wrong!

By the following June, not having had a single excursion in either April or May, I could feel the demons returning. I tried everything I knew to make the engagements more interesting, more stimulating, but it was impossible. Worthy and deserving as these charities and organisations are, they do seem to attract the dullest of officials; stuffed bloody stiffs in their starched bloody shirts. Nothing would do them but to extol the virtues of their own worthiness, their raison d'etre, ad nauseum, for hour upon bloody hour to anyone forced to listen! Whenever I was offered the champagne bottle to smash against something, I felt like asking for a massive swig first; dull the pain. I was consuming enough cheese and chutney sandwiches to keep the entire farming population of Somerset in gainful employment; scrumpy by the bucket! My morning mountains grew back, bigger, blacker and stronger than before. My moods became worse than ever. By the end of June, I was struggling; fit to kill. Hated my life. Had to do something.

July 1st nineteen sixty-seven, I awoke to find my bed perched on top of a mountain in the sky. It was snowing hard, a blizzard and a howling south-westerly buffeted the bed from side to side. One had to stay perfectly still so as not to tip over. Scared, terrified. Losing my mind. I needed rescue, warmth, my family around me; a cure. The doctor prescribed pills and rest and The Queen was informed of my mental anguish; didn't want to, of course, but I had to confide; simply had to.

She took it well, I thought, Her Majesty. Her husband was losing his mind, but she took it surprisingly well.

22

Perhaps we could do a time and motion study

The Queen and Prince Philip relax on a rare, engagement-free, Saturday morning … just the two of them on a day off from all official duties; feet up: an unencumbered, uninterrupted, lie-in. Her prince has surprised her and Elizabeth giggles with delight. A day off and a surprise assortment of chocolates and nuts. Heaven!

"Oh thank you darling… so thoughtful… I do so love a good nut."

She pops a Brazil in her mouth.

"So the doctor is concerned, Philip?"

"Yes, Elizabeth. I'm not sleeping well, as you know."

"A chill, darling? A summer cold? Not enough sleep? Can you fluff-up my pillow, please?"

"Not nearly enough sleep, Elizabeth and, one must admit… some degree of stress."

"Stress Philip? One is so surprised… surprised and upset. You have never complained before. I simply do not understand. What is this stress? What's happening, Philip? What *is* happening to my liege man? Surely it's not the volume of work. Edward is out of nappies, so there's one chore gone. You have your driver, your equerry, your own personal valet. You never have to pack your own lunch, and… don't touch that one, dear: the walnut fondant; my second favourite… and you can, of course, snooze on the way to appointments and again on the way back, if you so wish. We could shorten the engagements, one supposes; shorter speeches, pre-cut ribbon, easy-to-smash champagne bottles. I'm sure it could be achieved; a quick 'how-do-you-do?' a 'very-well-done', take the gift and home again."

"Quite."

"Quite? Quite what, Philip? I don't understand. Between the two of us, you are easily the more accomplished; we both know that. I'm the one with the slightly elevated voice and stiff presentation. You are so much more natural than I. Granted, Mother is better than both of us, but she's been at it longer. It's not that one… "

"I'm seeing things."

"Oh… seeing what things, Philip?"

"Mountains trying to break in through my bedroom window; black, evil, mountains; sometimes coming up through the floorboards, shoving my bed towards the ceiling; wind, snow."

"Heavens Philip, you mean like a pop star after smoking

one of those dreadful drug spliffy things? You haven't Philip; tell me you haven't… have you?"

"No, no Elizabeth, nothing like that."

Her Majesty sighs, then returns her attention to the box of confection lying on the bed.

"One needs to be careful," she declares, carefully selecting the next chocolate. "Never more than one at a time. Makes the most dreadful mess if one becomes lost in the sheets. But they are lovely, Philip; divine; thank you darling. Now may I have the coconut cream, please, in the corner. It's such a pity our guests don't think to bring more chocolate. One is sick of flowers."

"The doctor said I need to take more time off, dear. I was thinking… Tuesdays."

"What? All day Tuesday? Out of the question, Philip; poppycock! We are the British Royal family, not some… some… foreign royal family. We all have to work, dear."

"I'm cracking up, Elizabeth. Please try to understand. I may be very good at this job and it does have its moments but, it's getting me down. It's just too much."

"Pull yourself together, Philip. Where's the resolve? I ask you again. Where is my liege man?"

"I'm so sorry, dear, but it's simply too much. I need some time off."

Her Majesty licks sticky fingers, one by one.

"I see."

"… so?"

"One is contemplating, Philip. Perhaps we could do a time and motion study."

"Difficult, darling. Time and motion is more suited to… places like Birmingham."

"If you say so, dear. Exactly what do you need, Philip?"

"Every Tuesday, dear."

"Every first Tuesday in the month, maybe… until midday."

"Every second Tuesday, Elizabeth."

"Every first Tuesday, until six p.m., darling. That's my final offer!"

"Every first Tuesday for the entire day and other occasional days as necessary. The doctor has given me a note."

"And you will sign all the state documents, parliamentary papers and petty cash vouchers?"

"Yes dear."

"And the Christmas cards?"

"Those too, dear."

"In that case, one is not happy, but a compromise must be reached. One agrees, except for Sandringham, Balmoral, Derby week and Royal Ascot. Don't look at me like that Philip. They are enshrined in the royal timetable. No ifs, no buts, you simply have to come on holiday and racing. The public expects."

"Thank you dear."

"Not that one Philip. I haven't had the fudge yet."

"But you said never again, no more fudge; remember last time? Bellyache?"

"It was just a minor tummy-ache, Philip, and one is allowed to change one's mind. The fudge is always mine Philip… but, on this occasion, you shall have it. I do so want my liege man to be happy."

23

The holly would have to feature black berries

I was beside myself with enthusiasm. Every first Tuesday; splendid. What a woman, what a wife. Generosity unbounded. A full day off every single month. What man could ask for more?

One had to plan, of course. How far could one travel in the space of a day? Should I remain in London or take in the Home Counties, Scotland or even Europe? Disguised of course; that had to remain. Far too tempting for some abject criminal to take advantage of an innocent royal like me; totally exposed, utterly unprotected. And if, for argument's sake, I should happen to 'cop it', I just knew Her Majesty would be, quite rightly, very annoyed, and for a variety of reasons.

Firstly, let us assume I was murdered, ransom unpaid, of

course, and my body found with the usual degree of dismemberment, disfigurement and decay; not only would there need to be several days of official mourning, but somewhere would have to be found to bury me. Nearly all the good places are gone! Westminster Abbey, you say: it's so packed they're burying them standing up. Not at all dignified. And knowing Her Majesty's dislike for letting her subjects down, all deferred engagements would have so be squeezed in elsewhere, in her already hectic schedule. Logistical nightmare!

Secondly, given an acceptable length of time, a new consort would need to be found, married and run-in. More disruption; more expense! I have to be honest, do I not? It's difficult enough to train up one. Consorts don't grow on trees, you know. Worse still should my badly decomposed, if not entirely rotted body, was *not* found. Can you imagine it?

"Well, Detective Sergeant, is he or isn't he? One simply cannot perform one's duties in a state of unknowingness. Husbanded or not, sergeant? One needs answers, one's entire Commonwealth needs answers."

Thirdly, there could easily be a problem with the Christmas cards. On the assumption I was murdered and found early enough to enable the cards to be sent, Elizabeth would have to do all of them herself; no husband to fall back on. And which cards? Send the ones already in stock, with a live and possibly smiling Prince Philip, or order anew, with a dead Prince Philip, inserted at the side perhaps, or alternatively, no Prince Philip at all. And what of the Christmas message? Consistency has always been the key. Elizabeth would find it necessary to refer to her husbandless state, whilst not being either too curt or too maudlin. Tricky.

'My family and I, excluding my much lamented husband, possibly murdered – body not yet found – wish all our loyal subjects a very merry Christmas'.

As for the actual cards, the holly would have to feature black berries and fewer of them, instead of the more usual red and abundant. Not exactly festive!

Finally, the children.

Charles would be worried. Having two parents affords the opportunity to swan about the place, gathering appropriate titles and smallish countries, but if having lost his father, should Her Majesty, God forbid, also succumb to being dead, then the monarchy would be his. He would have to relinquish his new-found Welshness and become normal again. Heart breaking, I think you'll agree, after all that effort.

On mature reflection, it seemed to me that, if at all possible, dying needed to be avoided at all costs, so the disguises had to stay and if at all possible, be improved upon.

How best to prepare for my 'first-Tuesday-in-the-month' forays, you ask?

I'm not a devious man, you understand; simply practical. How could one be completely frank with Her Majesty? How? I simply must save her the anxiety that comes with having too much information. All married men know this. Considerate to a fault, I believe; a gentleman. If she had known I was dressing up and escaping down some noxious tunnel, she could easily have withdrawn my privileges. Best she remained unburdened by my covert, sanity-saving trips... for her own good. The trick was to be a vague as possible. Never *say* one was staying indoors, simply *imply* it.

"Oh no Elizabeth. One would not *wish* to venture outdoors in this weather."

"Study dear, and who knows where that *might* lead."

"Papers to sign dear. *Could* take all day."

Down the ladder, across the cavern, listen briefly to see if the Earl was in; occasionally, a brief chat; sometimes take him along; open the inside tunnel door, follow the passage around; check the cubicle was clear; open the heavy metallic door at the far end and out into The Mall; one's very own personal gateway to freedom. It felt wonderful to ease Elizabeth's possible concerns with my probable absences each and every first Tuesday of the month.

My routine quickly became established now that I had a bespoke day off, but not long into my new routine, events took a very unexpected turn...

Well, well, well and I laughed out loud

September sixty-seven.

Blasted rain; drenching: cats and dogs! Had to get out of it; one's only day off in an entire month and it was chucking it down. Mustn't grumble, I thought as I hurried out through Marlborough Gate.

I decided to do something indoors, to get out of it.

My wardrobe most definitely needed sharpening up. New disguises, I thought; one's old stuff looking a bit tatty so I sloshed up The Mall in my wellies, then availed of the excellent choice of public transport from Trafalgar Square. West End shops, I thought; Regent Street, Oxford Street. As a tramp about town, very important to look one's best. No self-respecting tramp can afford to be seen scruffy; one's attire slung together willy-nilly.

Great service, the London buses. The 7, 12 and 13; all very

regular. Ten, fifteen minutes, max., depending on traffic, you understand. I wished they'd introduced bus-only lanes; becoming frightfully congested. Alighted close to Selfridges and away I went accessory hunting; on the prowl for something… inexpensive. It was still early: nine-thirty. If I was lucky enough to pick up a new trilby or a pair of glasses quickly, I could carry on to Lords for the afternoon, assuming it had dried up, of course. Late season, but normally something interesting to see. If not, one could visit the cinema for a few hours, or perhaps wander into HMV to peruse the latest releases. Down Tottenham Court Road, there was a excellent selection of those new wirelesses and record players everyone seemed to be buying.

Just after ten o'clock I ducked into Woolworths. It was still teeming. No cricket today! Strange sensation being in a store, yet not being able to buy a blessed thing to take home. Must have had at least five pounds in my pocket. Burning a hole, let me tell you! An LP record to share between Anne and Charles perhaps, or a toy helicopter for Andrew; with moving parts. Chocolate counter; something small for Elizabeth; fudge was out! Bellyache, you see!

Alas, had to resist: put the money back; too many questions at the palace; impossible. I turned away.

That's when I saw the man who started my new career.

Gentleman; chubby chap, with a bowler hat. Aisle 5 on the left, saucepans, kettles, sundry home appliances. Noticed him as I walked along. Passé, you might think, bowler hats, but still quite common amongst the professional classes. Why he was looking at me in that manner, I'll never know. Hadn't he ever seen a bespectacled, red-haired gentleman wearing

Wellington boots before? And then he did it: quick as you like. Wide eyed he was; grabbed a saucepan lid, the smallest on sale: one and tuppence, and slipped it into his inside suit pocket. A saucepan lid! Well I never! Why? What good is a lid with no saucepan? Can't boil an egg on a lid.

What to do?

I looked the other way: out of embarrassment, I suppose. Quick-stepped away, up Children's Clothing and down Make-up. Looked across. Was he still there, the blighter? I ventured to the sweetie aisle; he went down Bedding. Perhaps I'm mistaken, I thought. He looked 'normal', and who better than I to decide. There he was; unfazed, except for his eyes, his rigid, dilated eyes: all pretence. He casually examined sheets and pillow cases: for suitability, I assumed: colour and texture. Picked up one, put it down, then several more; put them down; discarded. I pictured him in a neat three bed semi in Cricklewood or Wimbledon, suburbia; somewhere with bankers and accountants... and a bowling club. Not the Home Counties and definitely not foreign. He wasn't lost. But why steal a saucepan lid? Nouveau riche, perhaps, but not quite 'riche' enough. Librarian, maybe; wrong side of forty. Hen-pecked, most likely. Wife leaning all over him, for this, for that. Couldn't keep up with, you know, with the Joneses. Lost it.

He selected a packet of allsorts and proceeded to the checkout. I followed. Had to know; the rascal. Would he declare? Where's the lid. Nowhere; in his thieving little pocket, that's where... a shoplifter for sure. Straight for the door. Why did I do it? Couldn't stop myself, I suppose.

"Stop!" I shouted and he bolted. Lost his hat. Too quick

for him. As I said before, I'm quick, bloody quick from a standing start. Plenty of catches in the deep. Slammed the door on his ankle. He howled like a blabbering baboon. No sympathy, hope it hurts, you blackguard. "Hand it over," I said.

Amazing, but my disguise stayed in place: wig, glasses, cap; the lot. Only afterwards did I realise just how lucky that was!

The tea, afterwards in the upstairs office was most welcome. The manager smiled and I shook his hand.

"One lump or two?"

"You're too kind; one."

"Didn't take you long, once you started."

"Started?" I replied.

"Come, come… you're too modest."

"Just doing my civic duty, sir."

"Civic duty indeed. It is your job, after all, but may I say the explosion of speed to catch the culprit was very, very unexpected; pleasing indeed. I can see you'll fit in here. Now have you filled in the form?"

"When you say 'form', exactly which form are you referring to?"

"Blimey, do I have to do everything? The one in front of you, of course … there! Just fill in the bits that aren't already fully filled, and file the finished form in this fully filled-in form folder."

He handed me the form.

"I've got to dash. Delivery downstairs; needs checking."

He drank up and got up. A small man with an important air, he threw his chin skywards and strode out. Whoever this manager was – the nameplate said 'Hector Bellweather' – he clearly thought I was some sort of employee. Me! But how could I be? I was dressed as a tramp, all-be-it, a delightfully turned-out tramp and with, if I say so myself, a superior level of presentation and poise for such a position in life … not that anyone would care. And who, I thought, in their right mind employs a homeless vagabond straight off the street simply because he has apprehended a shop-lifter?

I looked around his office.

It was quite a normal office; modern; frosted windows, panelled doors; picture of The Queen on her own! No sign of me, oh no, not me: Johnny bloody Foreigner; just Elizabeth in all her finery and tiara; the glittering dress I liked, with the zip down the side. Nice photo though, similar to my own office back at the palace; more dust. There were hanging files along the back wall, drawers, chairs, pens and paper; a bin that needed emptying.

I looked at the single A4 sheet in front of me.

Application Form – Store Detective.
Grades one to three only.

My heart skipped a beat.

Heavens… a real job! He's asked me to apply for a real job. Superb; but wait. Reality kicked in. Impossible; out of the question. I knew how this nine-to-five malarkey worked. I was on a ship, you know: logs, reports, responsibility. Palace, full of them, household staff. What was I thinking? And why me? Totally unsuitable. I only had one day to myself every month and I wanted to enjoy myself. So much to do; to see. Snap out of it.

On the other hand, I thought, criminals; catching criminals, cripes... the challenge; crumbs, one could go for that!

Hector stuck his head around the door.

"Sorry old chap, completely forgot to ask; what's your name?"

"Ah, I... the thing is, sir... "

"Don't want to give it away, eh...? Mr store detective, but I'm afraid you have to. Otherwise, I can't pay you."

Conundrum. I'm a royal. One cannot tell a lie, except to The Queen, of course; but then all husbands lie to their wives, queens or not; have to; could ruin a marriage, constantly telling the truth. I lowered my head as if committing an enormous sin. When I think back, it was such a stupid thing to do, but I was on the spot, so to speak; I panicked.

"Duke of... Edinburgh."

"You don't sound Scottish to me, Mr Dukeof. Are you a Scot? Where's your accent from? Long way from the highlands, aren't ye, ma wee laddie, och aye the noo."

He laughed loudly at his own deplorable wit. Some people have no idea!

"Now start filling in the form. I shall be back soon," he continued.

I started to daydream. Surveillance; covert operations; chases up and down the aisles; rugby tackles; man against man; the fittest survive; only one winner. Been there before, you know; different circumstances of course: the Med. at night; enemy in the dark, Italians. War; equal measure, one remembered, excitement and sadness. Would my disguises hold up to the challenge? Ah … the penny dropped. That's why I'm here. I'm in disguise. He thinks I'm from head office or regional or somewhere; disguised; on the job. Well, well, well and I laughed out loud. The fun of it!

I looked at the application form.

Usual stuff. Name, address, experience, qualifications. At the bottom were the pay scales; grade three, five pounds per day; grade two, seven pounds and ten shillings; grade one, ten pounds. Excellent, I thought. I only get five pounds for the whole week from Her Majesty and she carries nothing at all, not a penny. You would expect Her Majesty to get something from the government; all that money they supposedly collect on her behalf; but no, her purse is always empty. Always paying, I am; tips here and there; could do with a bit extra.

Hector arrived back and I finished my tea.

"So sorry, Mr Bellweather, I really must decline."

"Please, Mr Dukeof, let's not be hasty. I could go to five pounds and ten shillings."

"I'm already in employment."

"Then why are you here?"

"I have Tuesday's off."

"I only need you once a month; rotation you see, you and the three others, the Tuesday detectives; regulations Mr Dukeof; compliance. It's good money… you won't get better."

"No sir, the offer is indeed tempting but… "

"Grade 2. That's my final offer."

"Grade 2? Seven pounds and ten shillings?"

"You should have seen who they sent last month, Mr Dukeof, a chubby bloke with a limp, and half blind. I'm desperate. You decide which Tuesday in the month. I have to make an appointment, simply have to. Regional office, you know; pushy. What do you say?"

"Seven pounds and ten and genuine promotion prospects?"

"Yes, of course; both long-term *and* secure. This is Woolworths, Mr Dukeof! Highly popular and extremely successful; people love stealing from us."

"I'll do it then. I shall, I will… first Tuesday of every month."

"Good man, good man. We start at eight-thirty sharp. Bring your own pen and paper. I like a full report."

25

New pingy-crisp or old saggy-wilted

"It's short."

"No it's not Mr Dukeof, it is all there. Didn't you read the terms and conditions?"

Mr Bellweather wore a silly grin, bordering on nasty, clearly enjoying my fuming indignation. You see, my first wage packet was somewhat lighter than I had expected.

What is it about earning one's first wage? Have you ever considered? Is it the pride; the independence? Maybe it's just the feel; the feel of one's own money in one's sweaty, touchy, feely, hidden wallet; waiting there, patiently, to be extracted entirely at one's own discretion, completely for and only for, one's own personal gratification; one's own whimsically indulgent whimsical whim; one's singular, covetous, greedy desire.

First pay packet. I wanted notes. Rolled up, wedged in;

bulky, tightly squeezed into my back trouser pocket; uncomfortable to sit on; substantial. Disposable income, hard earned and easily spent. Love money; love it; the nostril-filling smell of it. New pingy-crisp or old saggy-wilted; makes no difference; love it all. Hand it over Mr Bellweather, my palm extendeth. Caught three of those rascals for you today. Regardez-vouz, if you please, one very, empty, expectant, outstretched, ravenous hand!

"What do you mean, terms and conditions?"

"On the job application, you signed, Mr Dukeof; three months' probation on half wages.

"What!"

"Now, now, Mr Dukeof, three pounds and fifteen shillings; enjoy yourself; it's still a very good wage for just one day's work. You're far better paid than most here, let me assure you, far better."

He sat in his swivel chair, smirking, while I stood there, furious. But what could I do? If I could have given back half of my quarry, I would have, instantly. Looked at the form: inside coat pocket, just to check. Blazes to it. He was right. Three months' probation... wait a second, it got worse!

"There's only three pounds here, Mr Bellweather. That's *less* than half."

"Taxes, Mr Dukeof. We have to keep Her Majesty happy, do we not?"

He had no idea just how true that was. I sighed and left.

I dropped into the canteen for a quick cup and a sit down. All day on my feet, you know, watching and waiting, chasing and catching. I sat on my own and stirred my tea. Bloody hard to make ends meet, these days, I thought.

People think we royals are well off. Agreed, the accommodation that comes with the job is adequate, superior even, but the cost of heating the average palace is astronomical, a castle even worse. Try it for yourself if you don't believe me; draughty to hell. In your own house, think about it, you can close the front door; keep the heat in. In a palace, no such luck. Always people coming and going; staff, foreign secretaries, home secretaries, ministers, prime ministers, ambassadors, equerries, doormen, footmen, queens, dogs and children; doors always swinging open. And that's another thing; door flaps for the corgis; Elizabeth won't hear of it. Impossible, I tell you, but one has to put a brave face on it. I know what you're thinking. Allowance from the government. True, but believe me there's not much spare after heating a palace and feeding the horses and family. Need all the extra I can earn, let me tell you... lovely cup...

As I sat there, stewing in the awfulness of it all, Violet, a charming lady from Jamaica walked in and came over. She spoke with a heavy accent.

"What's up with you; long face, sir."

"Bloody Hector paid me short."

"I can lend you a bob or two."

She takes her purse out.

"Good heavens, no, thank you all the same; most kind."

"We all in the same boat, here. The Good Lord say, 'By the sweat of your brow'."

She sat down beside me.

"First day, is it Mr... ?"

"Dukeof."

"Isn't that a lovely name, sir... Russian? It sound Russian."

"Well, no actually, it's… Scottish."

"Well anyway, Mr Dukeof, surely you can take off the silly hat and glasses, now you finished for the day, Hector won't say nothin'. Your time is your own now, sir."

"Wish I could Violet, but you know… regulations."

I finished my tea.

Mustn't grumble, I thought.

Only had bus fares to pay; no rent or mortgage. My wallet had a nice 'little' bulge and I could choose when and where to spend. Nobody knew! And yet it hurt, despite my best efforts. The other man's grass is always greener and all of that. Stop it at once, I said to myself; must be positive; full wages in just two months' time… bloody Hector. The bus pulled away. Sat upstairs and looked around. The trip home took longer than I expected.

For all I say about him, Hector wasn't half bad. I'm sure there are worse bosses. He allowed me get on with it. I decided where the light-fingered brethren were most likely to target, not him! The sweetie aisle, absolutely: small easily hidden merchandise; household appliances, not so much. Much more difficult to secrete a coffee percolator under one's coat, or in a handbag, don't you think? Expected results, of course; told me so. Two or three a day, mixed, for head office, you understand. Had to catch a fair cross section for their analysis. Nab the blighters; into the back office; call the old bill; cart them off and start again. And a full report on each incident. Strange sense of humour though; Hector I mean. I used to watch him on the shop floor. Whenever he spoke with Tracy or Alison, he was all business, serious, but then he would amble up to me with his stuck-up grin on his silly little

145

face, and openly mock me. I was in disguise: of course I looked ridiculous. How would he like it if I grinned at him as if he was an imbicile? Bloody grade three Hector. And tight to boot; stingy! Still, one mustn't moan, must one? The plight of the working man. To be fair, must be expensive to run a Woolies. Had to keep costs down and that included me! It's not as if I hadn't heard those infamous sentiments before; indeed, from every PM from Winston to Wilson; 'We've got to balance the budget, Your Royal Highness… '

Not all negative, of course, working at the store. Hector could be most accommodating, especially with regard to one's holidays.

"As long as you work it in, my boy. Where are you off to? Oh the races, is it? The Derby *and* Ascot. Every year! Well for some. And Scotland in the winter; Hogmanay. Very nice indeed, Mr Dukeof. So you manage to get away quite often… with the wife… and the mother-in-law; that's a shame. Oh I see, she goes and you have to tag along, so to speak. We can't have everything, can we? I know, I know, I have no much say in the matter either. My wife, something similar. Hmmm, well, all those holidays, must be paying you too much, Mr Dukeof, och aye the noo; far too much Mr Dukeof, chortle, chortle."

Meanwhile, though I didn't know it at the time, my darling wife was making plans to find out what, exactly, I was getting up to on my day off…

26

"Bon voyage, everyone. Enjoy one's trip."

The Queen Mother looks directly into her daughter's eyes.

"Are you absolutely sure you wish to do this, Elizabeth?" she asks. "There can be no turning back."

Four women stand awkwardly outside Prince Philip's bathroom: a queen, a queen mother and two Ladies-in-Waiting. They huddle as one, whispering, as if protecting some slippery secret from listening ears and prying eyes. Anxiously they peer up and down the empty corridor, concerned somebody should suddenly appear and catch them loitering red-handed outside the consort's bathroom door.

"Yes Mother, I have decided. One is positive. One simply must know."

The Queen Mother coughs gently and speaks in a hushed voice.

"Is Philip away for the entire day?"

"Yes Mother, along with Anne, inspecting something in Scotland. Some sort of submarine, I believe; a Polaroid."

Ladies-in-Waiting look at each other. One of them ventures an opinion.

"But that's a camera Ma'am."

The Queen considers.

"I believe you are correct, ladies. It simply cannot be a Polaroid. No, it's a boat or a submarine my husband is inspecting. One should have paid attention, of course. He would not go the Scotland just to observe a camera. Heavens no; one can see so many of those in London these days. We even have one ourselves!"

Her Majesty taps her chin and bobbles her cheek.

"I've got it! Polaris; the Polaris submarine; silly me. Yes, very large, even larger than one's own yacht, you know: American. I remember now. It goes under water. Very keen on boats, Philip, you know; always has been."

The Queen Mother takes action.

"We've got to get on," she says, and steps up to the door, knocks and listens. There's no reply, only the sound of their own rustling garments and shuffling shoes. The Queen gulps and nods at her mum, who in turn opens the creaking bathroom door. All four dash inside as if playing a game of hide and seek.

Once inside, they look around. It's quite an ordinary bathroom. Tiled walls; bath and shower to the right; toilet bowl and wash basin straight ahead; railing with towel on the left. Had it not been for the royal insignia on the towel, it might just as easily have been a commoner's privy.

The Queen Mother points to a panel under the sink.

"That's where Jones said it was; directly behind."

The Queen looks to the Ladies-in-Waiting, hoping for some form of reassurance. Never in almost twenty years of marriage has The Queen had reason to question her husband's veracity. The very thought of her own shameful suspicion fills her with a vile self-loathing. Ladies-in-Waiting inspect first their fingernails, then their gloves and then their shoes.

The Queen Mother takes control. She strides over and begins to check the panelling. She bangs and raps and listens.

"This one sounds quite hollow, like the loose floorboard in the music room."

She runs her fingers underneath the cistern and finds a latch. Pulling sharply to her left, the panel slides away revealing a deep black hole. All four ladies look at each other. Tears well up in the Queen's eyes.

"So it *is* true Mother, every word; Jones and the Earl. One has been abandoned, discarded... marooned by one's husband."

Mutual sympathy envelopes the sad quartet like a chill London fog rising up from bowels of a wintery, windswept Thames. But the Queen suddenly stiffens and casts her head back. She dabs a damp eye dry.

"One has no time for self-pity. One must lead: oneself and one's people, whatever the trouble, whatever the strife, whatever the outcome. I am going in. Ladies-in-Waiting, I shall lead, you shall follow. Mother, you must remain, to stand guard and to tell the others... should anything... "

Ladies-in-Waiting stare into the dark, odious cavern and contemplate their privileged positions at this, their royal sovereign's hour of need. They look one another in the eye, as if to acknowledge that there are times when, perhaps they enjoy a little too much royal favour.

The Queen Mother offers a cheery adieu.

"Bon voyage, everyone. Enjoy one's trip."

She then opens her handbag, pulls out a lace handkerchief and flutters it, balcony-like, at the parting trio.

Down the darkened ladder they descend. The Queen leads. She pulls a flash lamp from her handbag and breathes a sign of relief when it flickers into life, for never before has there been occasion for its use. Light has always partnered the Queen; cathedral and castle, coronation and concert, civil ceremony and state affair; light has always shone on her glorious, smiling, regal face. But not here, not in the hidden depths of her beloved Buckingham Palace. Immersed in the stagnant swelter of the palace underground, a grimacing queen must provide her own illumination.

She follows her prince's footsteps, down the rungs of the rusty ladder.

The stench rises. Offended nostrils flinch in unison.

"What is that smell? The Queen utters, "Uuugg – some ghastly combination of decay and disinfectant. Goodness gracious! Remind me to speak with the plumber."

Ladies-in-Waiting begin to wilt. All those steps; all that effort; that dreadful stench; flies.

"How much farther, Ma'am?"

"Almost there, ladies, almost there. I can see the bottom. Chin up girls."

Her Majesty, in much the same way as her husband before her, leaps from the bottom step and lands in the same stagnant pile of sludge. Ladies-in-Waiting follow closely behind. All three catch their breath, whilst Her Majesty considers her next move.

"It should be here."

"What should be where, Ma'am?"

"The approved string, ladies. Jones told Mother that Philip had anchored the string beside the base of the ladder and that it will take one around the Earl's underground headquarters to the door beyond and that this is where the tunnel begins."

"The Earl, Ma'am...? The tunnel, Ma'am?"

"Come along ladies. No time to lose. Help me locate the string."

In the near darkness, all three search for the mysterious string. Slightly miffed, the Ladies-in-Waiting fumble around in the dark. Her Majesty has monopolised the torch, as if it were, somehow, hers alone. All well and good for her, she can see what she is doing. Silken gloves, previously white, are now covered with something decidedly unsavoury; shoes already beyond saving. The Queen also becomes irritated.

"Has to be here. Jones said."

"What's this, Ma'am ?"

The light beams on something shiny sticking out of the sludge pile. The Queen recognises it in an instant; a glass snow globe, the music box version, quietly performing its royal task as all royal snow globes do. The Queen fixes her light on it and three sets of eyes examine and find a Buckingham Palace balcony, full of royals, gazing back; all happy, all smiling, each waving to the crowds below, relaxed and contented under a glorious winter sky.

"Very clever, one's husband putting this to such good use, don't you think?"

She holds up the sludge-covered anchor and smiles contentedly.

"But Ma'am, it's... disgusting, covered in..."

"Not a bit of it, ladies. Very practical. One virtually trips over these, upstairs. I use them to play fetch with the corgis. This one is particularly galling. Look! Do you see? One is wearing a mauve hat with lavender gloves! Fashion *faux pas* ladies, and as for Philip, well, one cannot see *him* at all."

All three look closely; peering in the gloom.

"Oh yes. That must have been so embarrassing, Your Majesty."

"It was ladies, most upsetting. Fortunately only *The Sun* used the photo."

"But how do you know this is the correct royal snow globe, Ma'am, your husband's anchor? There may be others and it's so dark?"

"See here," The Queen replies, and tugs at the string which is tied to the globe with a bowline knot.

"Because of this, ladies. The string is royal green and made under my seal of approval. My husband would not have considered using an inferior string."

The Queen is now much brighter, knowing that her husband cares after all. He has used a royal snow globe in the stinking sludge and royal string to make good his escape to the outside world. If this is not proof of his undying love for her and the family, then nothing is! She glows with excitement.

152

"Come along ladies, we had better see where it leads. Isn't this wonderfully exciting? Just like an Agatha Christie mystery. I wish I had a corgi with me. There might be treasure or even be a dead body!"

27

Duuuum, dum dum duuum duuuuuuuuum

The Queen leads her expedition along.

"What if we get lost, Ma'am?"

Ladies-in-Waiting are less than impressed as they and The Queen trudge along, bent-over in the dark with only one small torch for illumination.

"Child's play, ladies. What could be easier than following a pre-determined path laid down by one's husband?" she retorts.

The floor is uneven in places, seepage having made some parts muddy and sticky; inconvenient, but not impossible. As for the flies, it's like the Newmarket stables after The Rowley Mile. The Queen and her Ladies-in-Waiting are occasionally hunched over because of the height of the ceiling, but following the royal trail is remarkably straightforward; Her

Majesty simply keeps her torch light riveted on the string, never once losing track until, some ten minutes or so later, the party happen on the Earl's underground headquarters. Of course, The Queen already knows it's there, providing the underground security the royals have to have, or so the Earl had said, though quite why one had not been informed until just three days prior was both annoying and mysterious. Nevertheless, finding the underground palace feels like a discovery, a wondrous discovery. Her heart lifts when she first catches sight of it, and though neither of her ladies comment at the time, she can hear their pants of excitement as they follow her lead... with perhaps the vaguest hint of exhaustion.

The underground palace looks like some sort of squashed outhouse, dark and gloomy, and sandwiched between floor and ceiling in this vast cavern. There's a rudimentary door and frosted glass windows on each side, with no curtains. A dim light shines through from inside. Imagine windows with no curtains, The Queen thinks; people can see in!

She turns to her companions.

"This is it, ladies: MI5 underground headquarters, Buckingham Palace."

"Headquarters Ma'am?"

"I know it may not appear to be much in the way of royal protection as one knows it, but this is a top level undercover facility, designed to protect the palace from all underground intruders. Who can tell what manner of deadly borrowing device might be used to assault the palace from underneath? I have been briefed by the Earl himself, you know. Twenty-four hour protection; precisely what we need, ladies. Top level at the bottom level, so to speak, to enhance the top level security we already have up top with a totally topping bottom-up operation. The Earl said."

"Yes Ma'am."

Music wafts through from inside. The Queen strains to hear. She looks at her watch.

"I think I know this tune. Can you hear? … It's the *Z cars* theme, or… darn, I wish I could turn it up. We mustn't knock. Is it *Dixon of Dock Green*? No; too early… ah… *Coronation Street* or perhaps…"

"*The Avengers*, Ma'am?" One of the Ladies-in-Waiting has come up with the correct answer.

Her Majesty replies.

"You are absolutely correct, my dear, well done." And she voices the theme music.

"Duuuum, dum dum duuum duuuuuuuuum; duuuum, dum, dum duuuum duuuuuuuuummmmm. I do so love *The Avengers*. Why is his reception so much better than ours?"

She has no time for answers, instead leading her tiny troop, around the corner to where the royal string ends beside a narrow door. There is no royal insignia above the door but she feels certain this is indeed the tunnel entrance. She turns the handle and the door opens inwards. All three enter the pitch-black tunnel entrance. An unnerving gloom bears down and for the first time, Her Majesty takes stock, while a quiet shiver runs down her spine.

"Perhaps one has had enough excitement for the day. Would you ladies mind awfully if we defer to another occasion?"

Ladies-in-Waiting look at one another and sigh an

exaggerated disappointment. They nod vigorously having already turned, heading for home.

Just in time they reach the bottom of the ladder as the torch-light fades and again, Her Majesty contemplates her predicament. Her husband still loves her, she thinks as she climbs the ladder; of this she is sure. But why has he chosen to abandon her, like some vagabond thief in the middle of the night?

Why? she wonders, why? And again she becomes dejected and morose.

28

Caught in the blinding light of one's own foolishness

The dawning realisation that her husband has chosen not to share the secret tunnel weighs heavy on Her Majesty's mind.

Gone is her exuberance to be replaced by a sad melancholy. It's late in the evening and she sits, slouched, at the far end of the table. How enjoyable it would have been to be part of his covert adventures, dashing away together, in disguise, to spend time in each other's company; carefree time, silly time... the way it used to be. The lights are dimmed, the room silent except for an occasional foot shuffle and The Queen's low sombre voice as she remembers better days. Her faraway eyes are strained, red, and swollen. The Queen Mother listens patiently, quietly nodding as she slowly sips a tepid, lifeless cup of Earl Grey; in her face also, the memory of a true love forever lost.

The Queen continues.

"I knew Mother, I knew from the very first. Remember at the college, the navy college, he pursued me in a boat. Father yelled at him, warned him to stop, but he insisted on chasing our yacht. I stayed on the deck and gazed down at him hoping he too was smitten. So handsome. You were there, Mother, remember? And he waved and waved and I waved just as much until the yacht pulled away and he evaporated into the sea, a tiny speck. Father didn't see but I blew him a kiss. And the letters, and the ships. Far away. He was brave. Don't you think he was brave? What man would have risked his life at sea, fighting the war and then, after everything, risk it all again; the most humiliating rejection if I had said no, or you or Father, and with the world watching and waiting on his every move; no parents of his own to advise, only Louis. Mother tell me. Was he brave for me or have I been an idiot, caught in the blinding glare of my own foolishness? He was the strong one, Mother, always so assured, and not at all vain. He led, I followed. Even I see the irony. The born leader and the born follower; roles reversed. Have I done this to him, pushed him away? What cost Mother, for queen and consort? What cost? Failed wife, neglected husband; happiness set aside for duty.

"Have I mother, have I failed him? What of our children? I know he loves them as he loves me so how could he disregard their needs for his own selfish pleasure? No, no it cannot be true. He is as honest, as kind, as supportive as any man could be. I chose well, Mother. Tell me I chose the best. I don't care what they say. One can almost hear the whispers. Fleet Street. I don't care. I never shall. Liege man, my liege man. That's all the matters. Rift. What rift? Let them prove it, if they can.

"I was cruel. He loved the sea. I knew and yet, I made him give it up. I was weak. That's why, Mother, that's why he has to run and lie and cheat and escape down a disgusting tunnel, making his way to… wherever he scurries off to. I have made him what he is.

"Am I talking too much? I am talking too much, aren't I Mother? Sometimes I do. I don't know what to do.

"Remember the day we married? Perfect day."

The Queen Mother nods in support and replies.

"Elizabeth, darling, you will have to speak to him. There may be a perfectly reasonable explanation as to why he…"

"Cheats on me. Is that what you are thinking, Mother, cheats?"

"No Lilibet. That's not what I was thinking. Perhaps he simply needs time away from royal life… from duty. You should contemplate asking him, simply asking him why.

The Queen considers.

"I know Mother, but I dread the inevitable confrontation. Even the suspicion that he knows what I now know might drive an even greater wedge; don't you see? I cannot… how can I? There has to be another way. Please Mother, help me find another way."

Remember that nice boy from the East-End?

The Queen Mother has a packet of digestive biscuits and feeds tit-bits to the eager-eyed corgis. She sneaks a furtive glance across the room to the French windows where Elizabeth stands checking the weather. Despite the heavy rain, Elizabeth decides she will take a late evening walk. She gathers in her dogs and picks out a sturdy umbrella. Her lips are narrow, her determined eyes shooting this way and that. She loses patience with one particular puppy who will simply not obey, whisking it up and placing a collar tight around its neck.

"Now come along, all of you."

"May I join you, Elizabeth. I have my stick and hat and it really is a marvellous evening."

"It is not a marvellous evening Mother. It's raining, it's dark, there's a gale blowing; but if you wish to get an absolute drenching then please come along. As for myself, I simply must get some fresh air."

"I know, dear."

Trees and shrubs billow to and fro as mother and daughter descend the steps to the garden. One or two of the less hearty flowers and plants have been uprooted and lie flattened on the sodden flower beds. Overhead a blanket of cloud unleashes a relentless, buffeting rain. Mother and daughter wrap up warm as possible and, angled against the appalling conditions, the pair decide to skirt the north wall first, then turn at the bottom and follow the path around. The corgis chase each other, frolicking, nipping, barking; oblivious to the weather. The Queen wrestles with an unwilling umbrella in one hand and a frisky pup in the other, failing in her attempt to keep herself and her mother dry.

She struggles to be heard over a howling wind.

"Oh Mother I wish… I simply wish I knew what he was thinking? Today, underground, one could not but be impressed by his courage, and his resourcefulness. But clearly he needs to get away."

She revisits her angst.

"Why, Mother, why? Have I been a bad wife? One shudders to think. I am despairing of what to think. I wish my love was not so deep, so intense. Is it another woman? Is this why escape has become so necessary? Heavens above, Mother, what am I to do?"

"Another woman! Really Elizabeth, the very notion is absurd. Your husband is a married man, in his forties, with four children and all the responsibility a man could possibly cope with. Why on earth would he wish to fall into the comforting arms of another woman?"

She does not wait for a reply.

"In any case, it's not another woman. Cannot be."

"Why not?"

"The Press, dear. They do have their uses. If he had been seeing someone it would have been all over the red tops by now."

"You think so? I wish I could be so sure."

A sizeable stream rushes by where a footpath used to be and a shallow pond now swamps the carnation beds between the lawn and the high wall. The Queen Mother rummages and finds a packet of unopened mints in her pocket. The rain eases a little and The Queen takes two.

"Don't worry darling Elizabeth, there are plenty more fish in the sea: Greek, German… even English. Not American, of course; one has no desire for a recurrence of David's affliction. What about that nice boy from the East End? Remember dear? What was his name? Was it Reginald or Ronald or something? One wonders whatever became of him."

"Mother! Listen to yourself. One cannot, after almost twenty years of marriage and with four children, simply change one's mind. Besides, I love him… I still love Philip even if… "

"Even if what dear?"

"Even if he has found… a new girlfriend."

Rain drops play with royal tears.

"I hate him, Mother, hate him; hate, hate, hate; deceiving treacherous, loathsome… how dare he? I wish he'd stayed in Greece or Germany or wherever he came from… I chose him, Mother, not the other way around. Why, I even pro… "

She stops mid-sentence, as if a secret were about to be revealed.

"I wish Father were here."

They re-climb the steps and retire indoors where Jones has a large gin and tonic and an equally large Dubonnet waiting for them. A Lady-in-Waiting waits with some warm cotton towels and slippers. They sit beside the fire, a quieter, calmer queen sipping and swirling the ruby-red liquid. She looks through the sitting room window and into the turbulent darkness beyond. The wind refuses to abate, choosing instead to lash and squall and uproot every living thing in its destructive path.

"He and Anne should be home soon and I have decided what I must do."

"Best to get it out in the open, darling Elizabeth."

"Out in the open? No Mother. That would be a disaster. I must allow my husband to find his own way, whatever the consequences. I will maintain my poise and stiffen my resolve. In due course, my husband, my Philip, will find the strength to unburden his cares and do his duty. Until that day, one must be patient, trust in God and trust in providence… and may I have another mint please?"

The two queens contemplate their respective positions, each sucking in silent unison.

Decorum dictates that one should never chew a mint. Every queen knows this. Dreadfully common to chew, and all those crumbling, crunchy bits, sometimes quite sharp, getting everywhere. Nor does a mint last as long as when one simply takes one's time and sucks slowly, massaging the mint firmly between tongue and palate; soothing; rhythmic. Finally The Queen Mother parks her mint securely near a suitable molar and speaks.

"Margaret is due over tonight."

"Is she?" replies The Queen. "That's all one needs … One wonders what trouble she has managed to unearth this time."

"That's frightfully unfair Elizabeth. You know most of the stories circulating in the press and on the wireless are totally false; completely made up. Idle gossip! She's very responsible for a young woman in her position."

"Come, come Mother. She routinely compromises the family. You know she does. Look at this Mother, just look."

The Queen pulls out a *Daily Mirror* from the paper rack. She shakes it out and fans the pages as if they were a tight deck of cards. A Lady-in-Waiting presents her with her reading glasses. Flicking through, she tut-tuts as she goes and nods and bobs her head from side to side.

"Pages three, five, six, nine and… twenty-seven, Mother. See for yourself."

Indifference becomes surprise becomes shock, as The Queen Mother thumbs from page to page.

"One sees what you mean, darling. Well, well, they didn't have such daring attire when I was a girl. Why one can practically see every inch… "

"There's no need to elaborate Mother."

Anxious queens suck and surmise, bouncing knowing looks back and forth with each fresh turn of the page; exasperated glances, pained and synchronised sighs; mints sucked too quickly.

Outside, the rain lashes the windows and saturates the lawn. What is one to do? The Queen thinks. One's nearest and dearest. So much worry, so much trouble. What on earth is one to do?

30

A queen, a queen mother and a queen father

Prince Philip has had a truly marvellous day, reviewing the Polaris submarine. Wonderful vessel, he concludes, a triumph in every respect. Shame, he thinks, he cannot say the same of his daughter. They sit together on the plane back to Heathrow Airport.

Odious child, he thinks, dreadful behaviour.

"I'm not happy with you, young lady. You've got to learn to behave. When a submarine captain says 'Do not push the red button', that's exactly what he means. It's not your cue to turn it into a game. Now sit up straight!"

Princess Anne crosses her arms and pouts. Prince Philip carries on.

"It's not good enough young lady. Have you any idea how

much damage a ten-ton nuclear warhead can cause? I accept you wanted to launch just one, the smallest, to see what happens, but you could have ruined the salmon runs for years or flattened the entire Gorbals. Basic manners Anne. I've a good mind to tell your mother. She will not be pleased, young madam. She may even take Scotland back."

The prince opens the complementary ten-year-old malt, pours a double and takes a much-needed swig, all the time launching dagger-eyes at his disruptive, immature daughter.

"Father, I have a question."

"Well, what is it?"

"Why do you dress like a woman?"

"What?"

"Well, maybe a transvestite or some sort of weird cross-dresser."

"What on earth… "

"I saw you do it, Father."

"Do what?"

"Last Tuesday. You thought nobody was looking, but I had a mentoring day, and I saw. Your bathroom, remember? You didn't come out, even when I knocked, so I knew you had to have an escape hatch somewhere. Wasn't difficult to find. You're so clever Dad, escaping down your… secret tunnel."

"Oh… ah… it's not what you think, darling; you see… "

"Are you queer Dad, you know, gay? Because if you are it's quite all right; in fact it's cool. I shall be the only girl at school with a queen, a queen mother and a queen father.

"Stop it this minute Anne. I've already explained. It's not at all what you think."

"Red wig, dark glasses, raincoat! Come on Dad! We did it at school. It's OK to be different. Are you a flasher?"

The princess leans back, folds her arms, half smirking but, equally, half dreading the upcoming explanation. The prince looks to the heavens, then bows his head and rubs his neck, deciding what he should say. Can she be trusted, the little wench? What choice do I have? The plane is only ten minutes in the air. There's no way out, no little white lie to pluck from thin air, to smooth-over the awkward, embarrassing truth. He grinds his teeth. Honesty, he decides, is the safest option, in fact, the only option. He exhales loudly and starts to unfurl the story of an unhappy prince-consort; a sad tale of frustration, depression and stress. Plenty of time to win his daughter over, all the way back to Buckingham Palace, but it's going to be a long, long, embarrassing trip home.

The plane touches down and they rush to the waiting car, trying to avoid a drenching.

"I had no idea Dad and I promise I shan't tell Mother, not a word. In fact I shall even help you get better. I shall volunteer for extra duties; anything equine."

"Thank you princess. You're such a good girl."

"In the half term, I shall do all of your chores and all of your engagements."

"There's no need, darling. It's really not that bad."

The prince relaxes in the knowledge that his secret will remain safe. As his transport glides along the M4, he pulls out the royal presentation package commemorating his and his daughter's trip to Holy Loch and, seated in the back, he's soon lost in the detail of an awe-inspiring Polaris. What it must be to command such a vessel; splendid, powerful, stealthy, unsurpassed; technically brilliant. The Russians would never dare, as long as we possess this feat of engineering, he enthuses; never; obliteration, k'boom. Think you're so bloody macho with your sputnik! Must order a scale model.

Now where did I put my pipe?

"Dad?"

"Yes dear."

"I love Scotland. Please may I keep it?"

"Of course, dear. It's all forgotten now, my very precious daughter, all forgotten."

"Thank you Father... did I tell you, I have a gymkhana next Sunday."

"That's nice, darling; local?"

"Buckinghamshire, Father and... I shall need some new things for the competition.

"Ask your mother."

"Mother would say no and somehow, I feel closer to you, now that we understand each other even more; don't we Dad?"

"What new things, exactly?"

"Not much really; a saddle and some new riding tackle... and all of my riding gear is getting too small and tatty... and a horsebox; Georgina has a much better one; and I shall need a new horse soon. Thank you Father. You are so good to me and I love you so very much."

Odious child.

31

One is not an eminence, one is a majesty

"Not a word ladies, not a syllable. I shall return in an hour's time. And remember, you know nothing, absolutely nothing! Now, I must hurry; time is pressing."

The morning is bright, The Queen happy.

Through the east window, a warming, welcoming sun illuminates the room and Her Majesty draws a satisfied breath. One or two carefree clouds take time to meander across the great London skyline. It's almost as if last night's worries have been washed away by the stormy deluge. Her Majesty has a plan.

The children have been packed-off in their various directions. Charles is already at Gordonstoun and Anne has just returned to St Benenden Girls after her trip to Scotland with Philip. The younger ones are safely ensconced in their respective nurseries till mid-afternoon.

Two Ladies-in-Waiting look on in a state of suppressed panic, their previous trip underground an experience neither wishes to repeat.

"Know nothing of what, Ma'am?" one of them enquires.

"I must again visit the underground palace, and speak with the Earl. As you know, one is not at all pleased with one's husband, trundling down that rickety old ladder and making his way, in the dark, all-be-it with the aid of some dependable royal string, to the tunnel underneath and adventuring, un-chaperoned, to the world outside. Something must be done ladies; one simply must do something! Therefore, I have decided to discuss the matter with the Earl, the underground Earl, and I must depend on you two ladies to deflect all enquiry as to my whereabouts. I shan't be longer than an hour or so… unless, of course, I fall over or lose my way or suffer some appalling, debilitating injury."

Her Majesty's eyes dance for a moment and she beams at the hilarious thought.

"That would be so funny, don't you think… if I fell… "

"Yes Ma'am… very."

The whimsy disappears from Her Majesty's face.

"Are my instructions clear?"

Having learned quickly from her previous visit, The Queen, on this occasion, wears sensible clothing as she scurries along the corridor towards Prince Philip's bathroom. Riding attire, bolstered by a warm woolly hat and knee-length wellingtons will protect, she decides, from the worst of the cold and the unhygienic conditions. Already, the absence of her constant companions has begun to weigh heavily, but the corgis shall simply have to be patient, and The Queen carries

171

on with a single minded determination. She ducks into the bathroom, slides the hatch back and as quietly and carefully as possible, climbs upon and descends the ladder. The metal rungs are cold on her hands and the odious odour again threatens to overwhelm royal nostrils, only this time, the pungent aroma has a more satisfying hint of bleach or disinfectant which she finds strangely invigorating. She checks the batteries in her torch.

Down she goes, descending steadily, rhythmically, foot following steady foot, until she reaches the bottom. Bracing herself as best she can, she jumps off and lands with a squelchy thud.

The cavern is as she remembered; soggy, black, foreboding. A swarm of winged insects arrive to welcome the royal visitor to their world, inducing in the Queen, a state of considerable anxiousness. The ladder back to the palace above, to safety, suddenly becomes inviting beyond words. She reaches out but stops mid-movement, for almost as quickly a belligerent resolve kicks-in and she finds her inner strength.

No worse than darned horseflies, she concludes, and she swats vigorously back and forth.

Becalmed and quickly regaining control, she checks her bearings and remembers the underground palace lies around the corner and off to her left, behind the centuries-old rock and foundation. Her torch quickly picks-out the royal string, Philip's royal string, and she follows it carefully away from the ladder up and over, left and right. The latter-day bread-crumbed trail enables The Queen to find her way through a Hansel and Gretel forest of concrete and stone. Much faster, she thinks, not having to wait on those fuddy-duddy Ladies-in-Waiting. She follows the string, manoeuvring steadily through the eerie underworld until, finally, around one last corner, and there it is: the Earl's squashed, underground residence. She knocks loudly on the front door.

Inside, a startled Earl, not expecting guests, rushes over to open it.

"Good Lord," he thinks, as he stares at The Queen.

"Your eminence, what an unexpected surprise."

"One is not 'an eminence', one is 'a majesty'… though now that one thinks of it, it would be rather a treat to be addressed as an eminence on occasion. One tires of the constant 'majesty this' and 'majesty that'. Eminence has rather a nice ring to it, one must admit. What about exaltedness, Earl? Do you like exaltedness?"

She carries on, not waiting for an answer.

"One has no time for idle chatter, sir. Please accept sincere apologies for one's unannounced visit. May I come in?"

"Of course, Your Majesty, but the place is a mess… last night's dishes… vacuuming, dusting. It never ends… "

"You don't have to tell me Earl," The Queen agrees; "upstairs one is forever brushing dog hair from the thrones and retrieving chewed tiaras from the dog baskets, but as I've said before, I have no time for idle chit-chat. One is on a mission of some urgency. I need to discuss matters which may affect not only oneself and one's husband but quite possibly the very future of the monarchy itself."

"Well in that case, please come in. You are most welcome."

Her Majesty is offered the same seat which Prince Philip had sat upon on several occasions previously. All around the

173

smoky sitting room are the trappings of a staunch royalist; portraits of the various monarchs in all their finery, the proud navy, the tireless army; assorted treasures of the Earl's homage and loyalty, big and small, scattered here and there and gathered piecemeal by her loyal subject over the many, many years. The Queens smiles in satisfaction. Father would have approved, she thinks. There's even one or two of Philip. Tea is refused, but fortunately, it's not too early to reluctantly agree to a small sherry from an unopened bottle. Her Majesty, not wishing to be rude, drinks quickly and accepts a refill.

"One's husband is escaping both his queen and his duty, facilitated by yourself and this… horrid tunnel."

"But Ma'am… "

"Do not deny it sir, one has seen the evidence with one's own eyes."

"Yes Ma'am, but if I may explain… "

"Sir, I expect no explanation, I simply wish to aid my husband in whatever way I can, for the benefit of the monarchy and the Commonwealth. If my husband is to routinely abscond, then it should be in a manner befitting his royal status, don't you think?"

"Well… yes of course Ma'am, but how…?"

"A final sherry and I shall explain."

As she climbs, a great deal more slowly, back up the long, long ladder, she thinks, with some justification, just how well her wishes had been received. But then one is The Queen she decides, and there are times when one shall put one's foot down and shall not be crossed. She smiles again, and checks her largest pocket, the gift of half a bottle of sherry, warmly appreciated.

174

Her Majesty reaches the top, catches her breath and listens. There are muffled sounds coming from the corridor, but the bathroom, she decides, is clear. She slides the hatch across and climbs out. Then waiting a moment for the sounds to cease, she quietly opens the bathroom door, slips out and scampers away down the corridor towards her own quarters. She has no time to lose. There are pronunciation lessons at one-twenty, ahead of the Sri Lankan delegation's arrival at one-thirty.

Below stairs, The Earl of Buckingham can hardly contain his excitement.

Recognition at last for the long lonely years of service; firstly with comrades-at-arms, now sadly deceased, except for Jones upstairs of course; and acknowledgement of his own selfless sacrifice whilst abandoned by his erstwhile masters, MI5.

Who knows where this may lead.

He allows his mind to wander…

My very own security division; treasury funding; underground anti-terrorism measures, anti-tunnelling devices, anti-personnel weapons of every description; equipment, guns, grenades, bombs, large and powerful… maybe even a small nuclear (all the rage these days). With all of this explosive power directly underneath the palace, he surmises, the palace will be safer than it has ever been. And yes, yes; an MBE at the very least… perhaps a knighthood. It's all too much to hope for. His daydream concludes with a seat in The House of Lords, humbly accepted as a token of Her Majesty's appreciation… Oh yes, and how I shall be ready, willing and waiting to explain to my eager and esteemed colleagues in the upper house, all aspects of under-palace security.

But first, the small matters at hand.

The Queen has been very specific and insistent.

Firstly, our meeting never took place. The prince must never know.

Secondly, Her Majesty has dictated a list of tasks which must be completed with the utmost haste and with the utmost secrecy. I must not fail her. I shall not fail her! Expense not an issue. Her Majesty has generously assured me she can supply all necessary funding: paper bags – beige; small denominations only, unmarked.

He looks at the hastily drafted list.

1. *Underground lighting*
   Bulbs; sixty watt to be installed at ten foot intervals between ladder and exit; royal string to be decommissioned. (Perhaps a small ceremony.)

2. *Flora and fauna*
   Fresh flowers to be placed, weekly, in vases along the newly-lighted escape route and supplemented by hardy perennials, leafy shrubs, ivy and 'that nice Japanese knotweed'. A frog or two to help deal with the flies.

Note to self – Check the Percy Thrower for shade-loving varieties.

3. *Bridge*
   Based on The Rialto: Venice not Dublin; to be installed over the stream. Small gnome with fishing rod to adorn.

4   *Tunnel décor*

Walls to be painted in approved Edinburgh Green (Philip's favourite). Spare statues, portraits etc. of the royal family plus royal navy ships, palaces, castles and a selection of wild life and foreign dignitaries (excluding despots) to adorn tunnel and tunnel walls, as appropriate. Mount royal insignia above tunnel doors.

5.   *Tunnel art*

Chauvet or El Castillo cave art to be acquired, perhaps both, and attached, as appropriate, to the tunnel walls. (Her Majesty to discuss discreetly with French and Spanish foreign ambassadors, ensuring enough remains in situ, to satisfy local requirements.) Second choice, if necessary; a small selection of locally acquired Elgin.

6.   *Sundry Other*

Two-bar heater and cushioned chair to be placed at the ladder bottom during the winter months. Fleecy gloves to be made available; fly paper hung; sludge removed.

32

They also serve their wives who stand and wait

Prince Philip again looks across the room to where the young therapist is seated. As always, she writes furiously, constantly updating her laptop, checking and double-checking. The whirr of activity both bemuses and encourages the prince to continue his trip down memory lane. Now where was I? he thinks… Ah yes, he remembers; Woolworths, wonderful Woolworths, and in his mind's eye, he winds back the years; back to when it was all so exciting, so fresh, so, how should one put it… exhilarating. He continues his tale.

Having spent, seven, perhaps eight months patrolling the Woolworths' aisles, I could feel myself becoming not only a fully functioning employee, but a proper Londoner; the man sat upstairs on the Clapham omnibus or in my case the 107 from Peckham Rye.

Woolworths was great and my disguises were holding up superbly well. One hesitated to acknowledge, for fear of some higher authority taking it all away, but I had grown confident; rounded; robust. And the job, not ashamed to admit: loved it. I was born to give chase, you understand; to apprehend and catch the criminal; some sort of giant hawk in a previous life, I expect. Heaven knows there were plenty to catch and, as I said before, I was bloody good at it. A one hundred percent success rate, unless I'm mistaken! If there had been a league table of store detectives I would have been Surrey and Hampshire rolled into one; opening bat.

I know what you're thinking. Big head… buffoon… prize idiot! But here's the thing, if you're good at something there's no point in denying it. That's false modesty in my book. Shout it out from the highest mountain. Be proud and accept one's accolade; that's my motto… unless of course, as in my case, circumstances forbid: circumstances being one's wife! Not allowed to upstage one's betters, are we? For me there was only the weary road of silent greatness, manfully trudged. Hector offered to put me forward as employee of the month, June sixty-eight. Had to turn it down. Impossible; no prizes for the supporting cast, you see. Who said it? 'They also serve their wives who stand and wait'.

Once word got around of my prowess in apprehending the light-fingered, they all wanted me; Brixton, Streatham, Wandsworth and Clapham High Street, I remember. Would have loved to, of course, but one had to be firm. I was only prepared to do the first Tuesday in every month, royal duties preventing any extension of hours. On average, one accosted four or five in a normal working day. My best ever was thirteen, but that included nine nuns from Somerset, all working together, who swore in unison that God had told them to do it. Their nunnery was in desperate need, or so they said. The physical search, to which one was not party, was a particularly difficult affair, according to Hector. In the end, soul-searching prevented the more usual body-searching and they were all let off with a warning.

The very next gentleman I caught in the act shook me to the very core and it took many hours of personal soul-searching to understand just why; quite a few pipe-fills of ready-rubbed, let me tell you, this nimble-fingered gent. Perhaps it was because I had become blasé, cocky even, I'm simply not sure, but upon my life, fully three quarters of the fun disappeared from that day forward. I began to question the simple pleasure of catching crooks.

He was mid-forties, slim, blond, well dressed but not showy. His clothes were well worn but equally well made, his shoes properly healed and polished. On his face he wore a world-weary scowl and on his greying, balding head sat a trilby, shading one eye: a throw-back to the fifties, and perhaps a better life.

He stole a spoon; a spoon I ask you, one tiny, single, cheap spoon. Only worth a penny or two, certainly not worth the risk. One distinctly remembers thinking he must surely have had on his person a hoard of other desirables. His overcoat, calf-length with lots of concealed pockets and his trousers, also pocketed fore and aft, were ample enough for all manner of temptation, but when I jumped him as he exited the main door, I quickly realised that that was it; a spoon, just one; a measly cheapy-cheapy spoon. No resistance either, no lame excuse, no panic. But he did look at me with the most amazing eyes: sunken and icy, barely alive, yet strangely intense. Blood flowed through them, I'm sure; they had pupils, corneas and irises: blue in colour, but no life. Normally one left it to the grade three Hectors in Oxford Street or Walters in Wandsworth, the Woolworth middle-management, do conduct the pre-arrest interviews but on this occasion I dived right in; simply couldn't contain myself. I asked if I could do the necessary… insisted actually, and the boss that day, a young lad by the name of Clive, somehow knew to humour me.

Shoplifters do not have to agree to answer questions, but most do, aware that it will probably lessen their punishment if they cooperate. This man, let's call him Trevor … Trevor Smith; he nodded in a sad resignation. Slowly, I took down the file labelled 'Goods Misappropriation' and looked around for a black biro; not blue, always black. He did not move, not an inch, while I sized him up and pulled out a blank A4. Who was this man?

"Name?"

"Smith… Trevor."

"Address?"

"Queen Elizabeth Parade, Streatham, South London."

Four children, a dog, a wife, a good job and a horse-share at weekends; a house, five-bed; holidays, public school for his children, a pension and an acceptable degree of social status. Established and establishment. He spilled the beans, spilled the lot.

"Why?"

I asked, not expecting an honest answer. I already knew

from his demeanour that he was a bad-tempered curmudgeon waiting to unleash some sort of tirade but he more than surprised me with his reply.

"I wanted to be caught."

Ruined my day and many more after that. The thing is, the thrill is in the chase: the primal hunger to capture, to overcome, to defeat. Hunting is fun, but catching a Trevor Smith is not. Kenya, fifty-two. Chased a wild boar; too fat to run; too easy; pitiful.

But there was something more.

Most shoplifters are like you and me. Big, small, fat, skinny and mostly bland They tend to think, if indeed they think about it at all, that they can get away with it; smarter than the system; smirk-faced and knowing-eyed, I find.

"Baby needs a new coat; no money. I know! I'll nick one from Woolies."

"I'm peckish. They'll never miss one or two little confections."

"Kempton races; fell at the first. The wife will kill me. Now what? An appeasement from Woolies!"

Of course, almost all get caught in the end. Just a matter of time.

Trevor Smith was different, not stupid, not bland. He sat in his chair, dejected but also relaxed, accepting. His differing signals puzzled me. There he sat, slouched, one arm dangling by his side, careless; but his intense eyes belied his casual demeanour.

"I'll lose my job."

"What about your wife, will she…?"

"Leave…? No; she'll cry a bit, run back to Mummy and

Daddy, stay a week and then come home. She'll hold my hand while she tells me I will always have her and the babies. Then she'll tell me I shall find another pensionable, secure, long-term, should-be-grateful-for job; start over, better than before... and what more could I possibly want?"

"You mentioned your job Mr Smith... Schools Inspector, I see."

He looked at me with those dead, defeated eyes, only now as filled with as much scorn for me as self-loathing for himself.

"Does it make a difference what I do? I'll be sacked as soon as this gets out; finished."

He had said 'gets out' as if he still cared. But equally he had said 'I wanted to be caught', as if he did not. Which was true? I found myself feeling immensely sorry for this man. I wanted to offer him an escape route.

"I might be able to help you, if on the form I expressed an opinion that... "

He became angry and jumped up from the chair.

"No. Tell the truth. I've had it with this whole blasted charade. Do you know what's it's like to be a fraud to yourself, to kow-tow to your wife's, your family's, your boss's, your children's every whim? Everyone owns a part of me. I have lost my heart and soul, and all for the sake of the safe, quiet, uninspired existence, week-in week-out, year after bloody, toothless, year."

He scorned himself and sneered at me.

"Why can't I live someone else's life. Anyone's! A tramp on a park bench has more freedom than I. Look at you with your silly disguise, your bland work-a-day existence? What do you know? You know nothing of who I am. Just do your job."

Later on, on the bus home, when I had opportunity to think through the whole episode, I realised he was quite wrong in his summation.

On the contrary, Mr Trevor Smith, I thought, I know who you are. I know exactly who you are.

33

Sling them in a bag
and trundle them home

Woolies is marvellous, don't you think? There's nothing one can't buy for one's palace or castle; universal appeal, I always think and so reasonable. Such a shame one could not take Elizabeth shopping.

My favourite purchase was a plant or shrub; always watching out for a bargain; not just at Woolies, of course; no-no; anywhere along the high street where the stock was half dead on some shelf near the back and where the Hectors of this world had decided to prune their losses. Tomato plants, begonias, lilies, tulip bulbs and the like. Pick them up for a song, sling them in a bag and trundle them home. Had to be careful Elizabeth didn't find out. Not a great problem really; plenty of room out the back where she wouldn't think to look.

Charles was always incredibly keen to see the new additions when he half-termed it down from Gordonstoun and later-on from Cambridge. As a boy he had magic fingers, still does! Dashed over to the greenhouse as soon as he arrived to inspect the new arrivals. Had forewarned him, of course. One of my great joys: Charles's ability at dealing with vegetables. Excellent with plants. Everything grew when Charles was around. The gardeners were always astonished at his prowess at resuscitating a decrepit runner bean or an ailing cabbage. Everyone commented on the size of his cauliflowers. Patient to a fault, he could listen intently to any conversation on any topic, however yawn-inducing and appear interested… like me, really…

Now where was I? Ah yes, Woolies … also marvellous for pictures and posters, the rolled-up ones stacked in the shiny, metal racks. Pop stars, flowers, animals; and all very reasonable. I've often thought of suggesting something colourful to brighten the palace up, not that there was much space left on our walls. We'd have had to take down a Rubens or Vermeer and move along a monarch or two. To be honest, I couldn't see The Queen going for it, so I decided not to take the risk. In this respect, home décor, Elizabeth has always been quite traditional.

I had been working at Woolworths for almost ten months. Time had flown by, as it does and I had established a regular routine, depending on which store I was assigned to on my first Tuesday of the month. I dislike the term 'store', don't you? Too American, I feel. Perhaps it's because 'shops' and 'supermarkets' are quintessentially British, just like me, but a 'store' is undoubtedly American. Does one really wish to become Americanised? I guess not. Alternatively, my unease at working for a 'store' may stem from the fact that the United States does not have a royal family; the Kennedys, you may say, but they're Irish; not at all royal. It's almost as if one simply does not quite belong. Now there's a feeling one never wishes to revisit: not quite belonging. Am I making any sense?

First Tuesday: I looked forward immensely to my day away. The dark, demonic experience of waking up feeling one's world was closing in, had alleviated considerably. When I awoke each morning, the mountains were still there; black and sheer as if to remind me that any escapade away from the palace was temporary; a mere respite from my gilded cage, but they had receded somewhat and reduced in size to the point where I felt I was regaining control. My moods were better. I arrived in time for breakfast practically every day. I was sane; alert; my eggs were edible; soldiers less chewy.

Now where was I?

Ah yes, my paying job.

One Tuesday morning, early July sixty-eight, I was approached by Horace, a bushy-haired Scot who asked me to join the Woolies trade union. They didn't have a store detective division, part-time, so I would have to join 'shop floor, senior skilled, reduced hours'. He was quite insistent and I took an immediate dislike to his attitude and manner. Unions, you see, not exactly my cup of tea; socialist upstarts; wanted nothing to do with them; pushy ones, even more so. Even if Horace had been the most polite gentleman in all of Scotland, which he was not, I could not see myself joining those dangerous blood-thirsty Marxists. Did he have any idea what they did to my in-laws? St. Petersburg nineteen seventeen. Did he care? I shall never forget. Had a good mind to give him a piece of my mind but, in the circumstances, thought the better of it. I declined his offer on the basis that I really did not have the time and my hours were too short. However later in the day, as luck would have it, I had reason to reconsider. Mr Bellweather called me aside.

"We have to put you on a productivity scheme, Mr Dukeof."

"Productivity scheme… me? But I don't produce anything, sir."

"Sorry old chap. Profits under pressure. We have to do a time and motion study, assessing the effectiveness of your performance against the company-wide demographic socio-economic diversity stratification findings, thereby, as you know, aiding the interpretation of the already extrapolated data and facilitating the introduction of a new non-seasonal age-adjusted variance to offset the already-known seasonal factors inherent in previously collected data. Look it says so here."

He showed me the head-office missive which, indeed, said just that.

"We also have to cut your wages by ten per cent… unless you can increase productivity."

"But I already catch all of your shoplifters. If I catch any more it will be people who haven't actually stolen anything."

"You mean achieve a greater than one hundred per cent stock-loss prevention ratio?" Hector asked. "Now that would be impressive."

"Yes, in theory," I argued, "but it would be absurd catching more people than had actually stolen."

Hector's eyes had already glazed over, his left eyebrow considerably higher than his right and a silly lopsided grin displayed a colonnade of teeth on one side of his face.

"Yes," he said slowly, "but if you did manage say, one hundred and five or one hundred and ten per cent, *my* store would be the most efficient in the country, even taking into account the non-seasonal age-adjusted variance."

"Don't be preposterous, Mr Bellweather," I declared.

"Are you saying efficiency is not important Mr Dukeof? That corporate goal-setting is somehow a devious head-office tactic to keep store managers continuously on an unstoppable treadmill of spuriously nonsensical target-achieving? Does non-seasonal, age-adjusted variance mean absolutely nothing to you, Mr Dukeof? You leave me no choice!"

Needless to say, I was not at all pleased and I told him so.

I went to see Horace and explained I had had a change of heart. Basic rights were important; principles mattered. We must stand together, shoulder to shoulder, and back to back, with our fellow workers, whilst we stride ever forward, side by side, in solidarity, up and down the Woolworth aisles, round and round the store in unison, taking a collective pride in our uncompromising principles.

"Pay cut?" he enquired and laughed out loud.

To my amazement, the threat to cut my wages never materialised. I became a union member and Hector had to be content with a mere one hundred per cent success rate.

That Horace… good bloke… excellent bloke.

Life improved.

One morning, shortly afterwards, I descended the ladder on my way to work, to discover the Earl had installed lighting all along my route. He was very pleased with himself and, knowing my Tuesday morning timetable, had waited to greet me at the bottom of my descent. Did it on a whim, he said, using some spare cable and lights he'd had from the early days. First the M1 and now this, I thought. One has to accept progress, I suppose, though I must say I missed relying on my torch and the royal string. Shortly after that, there were underground plants and shrubs and several frogs, hopping about. I thought the Japanese knotweed was a wonderful touch. One or two of the lesser shrubs struggled in the artificial light, but not the knotweed; wonderful shrub. Before long I had a little bridge over the stream, and a gnome; very thoughtful. Never got my feet wet after that. He then painted the tunnel walls in Edinburgh green and decorated with some strange chunks of stone covered in some sort of childish scratching. The stone appeared to be stuck on with glue. Carefully installed between the stonework were lots of pictures of Her Majesty, our children, The Queen Mother and George the Sixth, God rest his soul. I also had a Queen Mary, an Edward the Eighth and a Mrs Simpson, looking down on me. (If The Queen Mother had known there would have been hell to pay!) There were one or two frigates, several royal carriages and even one of me, looking in the wrong direction. He installed a shelf near the far door, with an empty vase, so that if I should avail of some fresh flowers from, say, a previous night's banquet, they could be put to good use brightening up that section and in some small way lessen the ever-present odours. All considered, a magnificent effort and I told him so. The tunnel was at least a half mile long! Then one Tuesday, as the days began to shorten, I arrived down to discover a chair where the sludge used to be and beside it, an electric heater by the base of the shaft. An electric heater! Had he any idea how much the electricity would cost? I unplugged it immediately.

All in all, one must say, the Earl had done a commendable job. Unfortunately, he would have to remain unrecognised and unrewarded. I'm sure he understood.

I looked around and pondered. It was truly amazing just how rapidly the palace underworld had developed over the past two years. Quite astounding, actually.

34

Just one little low-down, butter wouldn't melt

James Theodore Murphy was a dreamer. His dreams were his entire life from an early age.

At seven, he decided to be the first boy in his class to walk on the moon. At twelve he would play centre-forward for Celtic and at seventeen, having read Swift and Shaw while daylight faded, he would be the best writer ever to come from the Emerald Isle. But by twenty-seven he was living in London, eking out a living as a jobbing hack at The *South London Gazette*; dreams curtailed; ambition, brutally stifled. And now he dreamed only of a job, any job, putting steady money in his threadbare pocket. He plied his trade in the backwaters of Streatham and Brixton, covering village-pump stories of corner-shop owners and low level dignitaries; dull, dreary, depressed, workaday stories of the lower-incomed working classes. Pen poised, camera at the ready; take the photo, draft the gushing narrative and drop on the sub-editor's desk by five.

His refuge for the past six years was Mrs Kelly's bedsit, a Victorian conversion, just off Lower Clapham High Street. The bedsit was on the first floor of a narrow side-street terrace and was served by a communal entrance. Up and down the street galvanised dustbins cluttered tiny frontages, bored dogs chased mangy cats and dandelions decorated cracked and crumbling pavements. Cash only, she said; no questions asked.

Times were hard, but deep down Jamesie knew, felt it in his bones; success, a new life was just around the corner; if only… if only… has to happen: the change. Surely it will, he told himself, but in the meantime he had play the waiting game; the patient, plodding, painstaking, waiting game.

"Is that you Jamesie, at this hour of the night? I thought it might be a burglar."

"Aye, who else would it be Mrs Kelly, unless you've gone and re-let my bed… eh? Have ya? Have ya Mrs Kelly, re-let it on me? And don't you worry, there'll be no one breaking in here, Mrs Kelly; breaking out, more like!"

"So droll, Jamesie, so very, very, witty at one in the morning. Had a few on the way home, did ya? Where's me lodgings, ya cheapskate? You're all mouth and no trousers Jamesie Murphy."

"Tomorrow."

"That's what ya said yesterday, Jamesie, and the day before."

"Yeah, yeah… I'm off to bed. You'll get it when I get it, I keep tellin' ya that."

"Change the tune or I'll change the bloody locks. I'm warning ya, Jamesie. Had a respectable house before you came."

Jamesie climbs the stairs and unlocks his bedroom door. A muffled, high pitched Irish whine, full of a gnarly self-pity, echoes down the hallway.

"Never again… promises, that's all I get… know better next time… we'll see then Mr Jamesie Murphy."

He no longer bothers to reply.

Finally Mrs Kelly quietens and the house becomes almost silent. Someone, somewhere has a radio on.

Jamesie climbs into bed.

She's had plenty of rent from me, he thinks, plenty. He hangs his coat on the back of the door and kicks off his shoes. Six years in this kip.

From under the mattress he pulls the green bottle out, unscrews and takes a swig. He pulls back the curtains, opens the window and lights-up; takes a second swig. Smoking in the bed-sit is strictly forbidden so he only has the one and is careful to blow out the window. Nice few quid, he thinks, for the albino squirrel on Clapham Common. Had the photo to prove, along with the smiling councillor who made a solemn promise 'to protect the habitat of all ethnically-diverse squirrels' in his constituency. That's the thing. The *Gazette* will pay for something stupid like a wonky squirrel, as long as nobody else has it first. If I could do three or four of them stories every month, I'd be laughing. Thirty quid I got for that. Good money. The *Gaz* can cash in, he reminds himself; sell it on to the nationals. That squirrel, he remembered, ended up in the *Mail* and the *Mirror*; nice few quid but not enough, not by a long chalk. Keeler's mate who didn't know anything paid a bit; should have been more, and the bent copper who surprised everyone by being straight. That diamond little tale coughed up near a score. But that was it in a whole six months. Need a biggie, a nice, plump, juicy biggie. A royal big-wig or a crooked politician; that would do; that's where the money's at; the readies. There's always dirt on the royals but it's hard to sniff out. Get a staff job for sure if I could get just the one little scoop on that lot… just the one little low-down, butter wouldn't melt, on one of them; any of them. I'll take anything. Not fussy; drugs, drink, brown bag, anything… even sex, God forgive me.

Not The Queen, though. None of the papers would touch that. Anne or Margaret would do; maybe Anne's too young. What age is she? The Queen Mum might do. Something hushed up from the past, or The Queen's husband, what's-his-name, the Greek bloke… or is he German? Ear to the ground, me mate Phil says; should hang around the palace. Something's bound to crop up sooner or later with all them royals wandering in and out. But I could wait forever; that's the problem… Maybe Phil's right; patience. Who-the-feck knows? A few quid to a housemaid or butler, maybe; spill the beans; then I'd be in gravy. Elsie wouldn't say no then, would she? Christ no. Classy bird, Elsie, but no hope with the money I'm on. Barely pay the lodgings. Have to make do with Marcie and her stinky cats. Cheap as chips, Marcie. Doesn't look good in that mini; someone should tell her; but I wouldn't risk it. Do for now, I suppose.

What day is it? Monday. Tomorrow, early start; hospital

extension at Cheam. Tree-planting. Get the photo, take the leaflet and write it up. No much money, but the car needs petrol. Then, let's see, bus it up the city after lunch; the boss needs new photos for next week's feature. Meet up with Marcie. Her place.

Jamesie puts the bottle to his lips for one final swig, screws the cap back on, and shoves it under the mattress. If Mrs Kelly knows, she says nothing.

35

He was too close: smelled of bilge and body odour

First Tuesday of the month over, I caught the first bus home from work, the dependable 139. I adjusted my new wig for the umpteenth time: the one I'd purchased specially for Woolies; 'Strawberry Blond' in the catalogue. Nice shade; made me look like one of those hippie types; also available in auburn and chestnut. Went excellently well with the 'country fair' tweed jacket, the obligatory dark glasses, mustard riding breeches and black brogues. In my line of work, it paid to be well-presented, you understand; co-ordinated.

Damned thing didn't fit properly; the wig, I mean. I pushed and pulled at it all day long; a tad small, you see. Had to use lots of Elizabeth's hair clips and even then it meandered all over my head. Needs must, I simply had to be more careful. Stiff-necked it all day, I remember. More difficult to catch the blighters when one cannot move one's head, but I still managed my usual quota, one hundred percent.

As I've said, I sat upstairs on the bus, halfway down, surveying my wife's realm. I liked being up top, watching the world go by. I bent over to tie a shoelace and some idiot grammar school lout charged past me sending both wig and glasses flying. Having briefly uttered some appropriate rebuke, I rapidly gathered-up my scattered disguise, sorted it out and put everything back as best I could. Short several hair clips, I recall. Had to be quick. Looked down the bus to see if anybody had recognised me. There was an Asian group crowded together, giggling and tittering: tourists, and a bloke in a crumpled trench coat, head lost in a broadsheet, and a woman in curlers with her toddler, about Edward's age. What was she doing with a toddler upstairs? Silly girl. None of them paid any attention. I was in the clear. The idiot schoolboy apologised, as indeed he should. Narrow escape, or so I thought.

I made my way down The Mall, having disembarked at Trafalgar Square. Then out of my peripheral vision I noticed a bedraggled man in a long, shapeless coat hotfooting it after me. I was being followed. Drat! Was he on the bus? Must have been. Which one? Makes no difference now. My navy training kicked in and I adopted diversionary tactics. Took a ninety degree to starboard doubling back to aft and then tacked hard-a-port, between park bench and park bushes. He followed, the blackguard… crumbs, that didn't work! I tried a head-on confrontation; walked straight at him, with purpose. He pretended he was not following and began whistling to the clouds and adjusting his tie but as soon as I walked past him, he turned and again started to run, flapping a notebook in the air.

"I know who you are, sir," he called out, in some sort of accent: Irish, as it transpired.

Darn it to hell; trouble!

I ran for it, over flower beds, bushes, behind trees, benches; around litter bins, like a hare. I didn't know what I was doing, scurrying as best I could towards safety. Dogs yelped, ducks and pigeons scattered; squawking and squealing. I've panicked. He's followed, but he's no quicker than I. We're scurrying around like something from an episode of Benny Hill.

"Stop or I'll shout out your name!" he yelled.

The game was up. I did as he demanded; panting; not a young man anymore, you understand. Quite good over the short distance, like in a Woolworths store up to, perhaps, fifty yards, but ask me for stamina, could no longer do it, couldn't run anymore. We've ended up close to the café where my tunnel meets the outside world, both of us gasping for breath. I gestured to an empty table beside the café, all the time scanning for a possible escape route, working out what to do; but in truth, I had no idea. I was in a proper fix; needed time to recover and think.

"Well, well, well, what have we here, Your Royal Highness *in disguise?*"

His words were slow, deliberate, triumphant. He'd clearly caught his breath. He was younger than I and the way he emphasised the words 'in disguise', full of scorn and nastiness, spelt trouble.

"You're mistaken. Why are you chasing me?"

He indicated a policeman, sauntering near the St James's Park lake, hands behind back, classic mode, clearly enjoying his evening amble.

"Will I call him over for you, sir? Will I?" He grinned and sneered as he straightened his greasy tie. His teeth were ghastly; same colour as his tie: earwax yellow.

"You've no idea how long I've waited, Prince… em… "

"What do you want, you scoundrel," I retorted under my breath, "and it's Philip."

"Let's stay calm, Your Royal Highness, have a coffee and talk it through," he whispered in reply. He was too close; smelled of bilge and body odour.

The evening was cold, but when the coffee arrived, it most certainly took the edge off the chill. He paid. Least he could do. He gulped his like a man deprived, splashing and re-staining an already pockmarked overcoat. I drank mine more slowly. Neither of us sat comfortably; he, faced with the biggest moment of his, no-doubt, lamentably sorry career and I, trying to concoct an escape.

The Med. all over again; needed to create a diversion, effect an escape and bloody quickly!

36

We must marry British, next time

Jamesie had struck pay dirt. His wide eyes jumped in excitement, for across the table sat none other than Prince Philip, captive and in disguise.

He leers at his quarry, his coffee cup shaking in his hand. I've got him, he thinks, a feckin' prince, a feckin' big-wig, real life prince. Clover! Holy Mother of God, Jesus Christ, I can't believe it. Wait till this gets out. Scoop of the frigin' century. World rights. Set-up for life… Elsie!

Headlines jostle for space in his mind's eye: all of them front page;

PRINCE PHILIP IN SHAMEFUL DISGUISE SCANDAL
TEARFUL QUEEN DABS MOURNFUL EYE
HANGING TOO GOOD
PM AGAIN QUESTIONS IMMIGRATION POLICY

Don't blow it, he thinks. Don't be an eejit. Stay calm; he's in the bag. Got to get this right. Ok. No need to abuse the royal gentleman. Be respectful; best way. Yeah, here's what I'll do; give him two choices; the easy way and the hard way.

The coffee dribbles down his chin and onto his shirt and tie, but he doesn't notice, his eyes fixed dead ahead.

Where's my notepad, he thinks, and my pencil.

Got to get this right…. oh yes… for God's sake, don't screw it up!

37

What happened next was, believe me, totally unbelievable

I sat quietly in my chair, waiting, slowly sipping my coffee. At that moment in time, there was absolutely nothing else one could do. The dishevelled creature in front of me took out his notepad, wiped his mouth on his sleeve, sniffled, sniffed and spoke.

"Prince Philip, Your Royal Highness, we can do this the easy way or the hard way. Which would you like?"

"Easy or hard?" I replied.

"'Easy' and I take your photo, with and without, and I will allow you sir, to tell me why you are in disguise. Our interview will be sympathetic; let me see; the anguish, the pressure, the pain, how fully supportive you are of The Queen, the Commonwealth, etc. etc.; loving family man. Just a blip on an otherwise stainless career, sir. 'Hard', and I take your photo, with and without but as you have sulked and not told me what I need to know, I shall be forced to make up 'the terrible truth of a royal rat'; Prince Philip; heartless, vile, ungrateful refugee, taken-in in his hour of need and now, disloyal, undeserving etc. etc. How The Queen must rue her choice of consort… hanging too good."

"Can you repeat the choices," I replied.

He did not appreciate my sense of humour and rose to see where the policeman was.

"Sit," I said, accepting my fate. "'Easy', of course. Now what would you like to know?"

"Let's start with a photo, Your Highness."

He took out his camera; one of those new thirty-five millimetres with wide-angle lens; too good for the likes of him.

"And smile, if you please."

I obliged. Ironic, you know: first proper photo taken of me in years.

"Now sir, let's have the disguise off for the next snap."

"Don't be silly, too many people. You'll cause a riot. We shall wait till the end, when it's quieter."

He looked at me intently, trying to work out if I was stalling for time or was, surprisingly given my current circumstances, simply courteous and helpful. He looked around. Fortunately there were quite a few tourists, many with cameras, and I'm sure the thought occurred to him that if he insisted, several others would also avail of the opportunity to capture the royal image, any of which could have easily been sold in advance of his. I could see he was unsure. He rubbed his chin, straightened cuffs that had never previously been straight, and eyed me several times before reluctantly nodding.

"We'll do it at the end then sir, with the flash, when there's no one else around."

I exhaled very, very slowly and leaned back in my chair.

He flipped over the cover of his dog-eared notepad and began to write. From where we sat, the tunnel, my safe haven, was only twenty yards away. Somehow I had to make it over, but how?

What happened next was, believe me, totally unbelievable.

Walking towards me and heading directly towards the men's toilet, were Lord Lucan and Ronnie Biggs. They had matching wigs, 'natural tan de-luxe', unless I'm mistaken; both cheaper and tackier than mine. No surprise there. They both wore dark glasses and false moustaches. Biggs had spats; Lucan, a cane walking stick. Up to no good, I thought. They stopped for a moment and looked around slowly to check if they were being followed. They then turned and walked briskly into the toilet. A plan leaped into my mind just as my adversary was about to commence his interview.

"I need to go to the toilet," I announced.

"You'll make a run for it."

"Shan't. I promise and I'll give you an excellent interview when I get back; scout's honour."

"Scout's honour?" he repeated. "Alright then. Don't be long and don't try anything funny. That copper is still over there," and he pointed his finger. "I'll be watching."

I went straight to the convenience.

Lucan and Biggs stood, side by side at the wash basin, deep in hushed conversation.

"You've been spotted," I said, trying to sound like a commoner, "by the plainclothes copper outside. I'll sell one of you my disguise for twenty quid."

Biggs dashed to the door to have a look, peeking towards the table where my Irish interrogator sat compiling his questions. In an instant the great train robber returned and belted Lucan with a solid right, dispatching him to a quieter, happier, more sedate place. So much for honour among thieves.

"Gimme the gear," he said. I chose not to argue.

He flung a twenty at me and grabbed my wig and glasses. I'd have taken ten.

"Boots and coat," he growled.

I obliged and he wasted no time, shoe-horning himself into my disguise. He looked at me, goggle-eyed, as if he recognised me vaguely from somewhere, before returning to the serious business of escaping.

Lucan moaned and Biggs lamped him again, before whipping off his moustache: his own, not Lucan's; no point in that. Decked out as me, he walked out briskly, and up towards Marlborough Gate, hoping, one supposed, to blend into the crowd and make good his escape.

"Oi, come back you, or I'll… "

The Irishman had spotted him.

Biggs bolted; taking off like a skittish gazelle from a ravenous cheetah. My Irish persecutor also scrambled away in hot pursuit, skittling tables and chairs in his wake. Never was I so pleased to see a criminal on the run. Down The Mall Biggs dashed, towards The Arch; legs like pistons, the Irishman flailing behind.

"Stop, stop, Your Royal Highness; scout's honour sir; what about scout's honour sir? Stop. I'll call the police, I'll call the coppers... "

At this point, a man, probably a tourist, rushed into the gents, clearly in need, but confronted by an unconscious Lord Lucan in the arms of a near-naked royal look-a-like, he decided he had an even greater need and reversed out again... quickly!

I put on the discarded Biggs disguise and pondered what best to do with the comatose Lucan. One felt quite sorry for the fellow, despite his reputation as an inveterate gambler. Obviously, I could not take care of him myself, so I decided to allow the underground Earl the pleasure. I hauled him into the tunnel and laid him out just inside the entrance. He was out cold and a dead weight. Plenty of time, I decided, for the Earl to come down, bind and gag him, before deciding how best to either release him or take him to the police. Lucan, despite being throttled, looked peaceful, I thought; contented.

Slept soundly myself that night, I must say; A hack bamboozled, six assorted shoplifters apprehended at Woolies and twenty pounds better off. Life hadn't been so good for some considerable time. Just one regret, however; the scout's honour; not the gentlemanly thing to do, you understand; but, I simply had no choice, did I? Bloody hacks.

The Queen, as I subsequently discovered, had not been quite as contented as I. No indeed.

Quite the reverse, it transpired! Her Majesty was decidedly unhappy.

38

One should never visit the Netherlands before October

"How long has it been, Mother?"

"Pardon dear. How long has what been? Have you seen my curlers?"

"Haven't I been immensely patient with him? I have waited and waited, hoping, wishing, praying, but in truth I am no farther forward than this time last year. They're over there Mother, look... beside the shawl... under the tiara... not my tiara, yours... next to the sceptre."

"Ah, yes, thank you darling... you mean Philip? What's the matter now?"

"He's still disappearing down that horrid tunnel, regular as clockwork. Thinks I don't know; pretending to go to his study; skiving off to wherever he goes; not a care in the world.

Must be another woman, Mother; simply has to be; some shockingly seedy boudoir in Kensington or Knightsbridge, all pinks and reds, floppy and soft… disgusting."

"There, there, Elizabeth, how can it be another woman? He's much too happy."

"Do you think so?"

"Haven't you seen how jolly he is, Elizabeth: always spruce, full of that joie-de-vivre the French invented; plays with the children, reads bedtime stories, does his chores with a big smile on his face. I've seen it myself. No it can't be a woman."

"He is remarkably happy, one must admit; disconcertingly so. When I said we were to tour Brazil and Chile in November, one fully expected the sulks; you know how he can be, but no, he simply smiled and nodded and said he should have the next available Tuesday instead. It's ridiculous, Mother. Why is he so happy? It's not normal. Royals simply do not *do* happy. Demure, yes; happy, no. I shall have to speak with him, to explain if necessary, and ask him to curtail. What if the press were to find out?"

"Try to be reasonable, Elizabeth. It may be an illness, this excessive happiness."

"I suppose so, Mother, but none of the other royals ever suffered from it. Did Father, or George or Queen Mary? Victoria wasn't even amused. Except Edward, of course. He was one of us. Then it happened to him when he met that awful Mrs Simpson. Lost his crown over it! Got to be so careful. Look at any of the portraits. Look at my stamps. Not a hint of happy. Moderate joy on special occasions, of course, but rigidity, irritability, sternness; that's what's needed; always has been. Even a smile must be used sparingly. The public expects royal reserve and we must expect to be expected to satisfy their expectations. Granted, one sees this unfortunate manifestation quite often among the commoners. Whenever I come along, they simply burst out in fits of happiness, irrespective of the occasion. And not just for me, as you know. Any minor royal will do. All one has to do is wave. Where do they get it from, this… glee? One is not sure which is worse among one's subjects, the uncalled-for and excessive mirth or that other compulsion: to rip-up every flower for miles around and strangle them into presentation bouquets; bewildering. And abroad too. One should never visit the Netherlands before October."

"Yes I quite agree Lilibet. Margaret used to suffer from too much happiness, if you remember, but she's a proper royal now. So what shall you do?"

"Carry on as normal, of course. Just the right amount of mirth."

"No, not you dear, I mean Philip, your husband."

"Oh him!"

The Queen sighs.

"One is so unsure Mother. Perhaps one depends on the other. Negate whatever it is on the far side of that horrendous tunnel and God willing, the excessive happiness may also be cured."

"I agree dear. Do what's best. Now where did I leave my broach? Did I have a broach? Has anyone seen my broach?"

"Try the dog basket, Mum. If it's not there, I'll send Jones to The Tower for something."

Tea arrives.

Mother and daughter sip in silence. Finally The Queen speaks.

"I have reached a decision, Mother. One cannot wait another moment. I shall have to follow him and find out for once and for all. Tomorrow morning, while Philip hosts the wild animal people to discuss their habitat, I shall pay a visit to the underground Earl and decide the best approach. I love my husband so much Mother, as you know, despite his tardiness and excessive joy and shall do whatever it takes to retrieve him, my wonderful Philip; make him normal again. I shall instruct Jones to make the appointment immediately."

Next morning, The Queen descends into the depths.

The ladder down is just as steep as she remembered, as is the dreadful odour and the bothersome winged insects; ghastly, but what a pleasant surprise when she jumps off at the bottom. There to greet her, with a bouquet of almost fresh flowers is the underground Earl. The sludge pile has gone and there's a heater nearby, unplugged, and a chair with a cushion. The cavern is lit up, like some lacklustre fairy tale grotto; dim and unpretentious, with some dark unnerving shadows; sixty-watt bulbs trying their best. There's a proper pathway, in London brick, leading all the way along to the Earl's underground palace and presumably beyond, to the tunnel entrance. The Queen is very pleased at the Earl's diligence in carrying-out her instructions. She both smiles *and* nods. There are vases at intervals festooned with drooping but still perfectly acceptable flower arrangements and there's an array of shade-loving foliage on either side of the pathway. The Queen notices with pleasure, as had Philip, how well the Japanese knotweed has adapted, but she has no time for excessive pleasantries and the pair adjourn to the Earl's sitting room.

"One's husband continues to escape; every first Tuesday and I suspect at other times too."

"This is true, Ma'am. I must confess I have accompanied him on occasion, purely in a security capacity you understand, but never on a first Tuesday. He appears to have a personal agenda for his first-Tuesday forays and I'm afraid, I am not privy."

The Queen becomes annoyed.

"And what of the trips to which you *are* privy? What have you… men-about-town been getting up to? Well? Gambling, drinking… womanising?"

"Great Scott no, Ma'am. We simply behave as normal people; sightseeing; afternoon matinees; pizza."

"One has never had pizza."

"Marvellous food Ma'am, Italian… nourishing in its own way, they say; Waldorf Street."

"Nourishing? You mean like porridge?"

"Not exactly Ma'am."

"What of Tuesdays, Earl. Where does he go? You had better not lie!"

"I have no idea Ma'am, I promise."

The Queen regards him with narrow-eyed suspicion.

"Then we shall both follow him next Tuesday. I shall cancel all appointments. Bang loudly on the ladder two minutes after he has gone. Be ready in full disguise. We shall follow him and find out once and for all. Good day sir."

The bare-faced cheek of it, saying 'good morning' to a married man

As a mother and a queen, one was used to being up early, but that particular morning, one was up extra early, selecting appropriate garments, applying make-up, and getting oneself ready for the momentous day ahead. A Lady-in-Waiting assisted, both in deciding one's dress attire, and in checking that the proper effect was achieved. Between us, I remember, we decided on rollers in my hair, a headscarf, comfortable blouse, knitted cardigan, jodhpurs and sturdy knee-length leather boots. We chose a suitable handbag, with a fold-away umbrella in case it should rain. Dark glasses were selected, and a pair of gaudy gold earrings completed the ensemble. My Lady-in-Waiting remarked, with some small justification, that one was charlady from the waist up and three-day eventer from the waist down. She found it amusing, I did not.

I waited for Philip to sneak along the corridor to his bathroom then listened outside until I heard him slide across the shaft door and descend the ladder. I almost turned back, ashamed of myself for what I was about to do but I forced myself to continue, to overcome; the lesser of two evils, you understand; simply had to find out.

At the bottom, the underground Earl greeted me.

"You look wonderful, Ma'am, delightful."

His observations were both unnerving and unbecoming, but moderately flattering nonetheless.

"One most certainly does not, sir! One is in disguise and please refrain from making personal remarks."

"Apologies Ma'am."

The Earl was also heavily disguised. He wore a business suit: black-striped, black shoes, sombre tie as befits a city gent and he sported a big black bushy beard which was somewhat at odds with the rest of his outfit. The attire was finished off with a black bowler hat and the obligatory dark glasses; quite a handsome man, in a certain light.

"We have no time to lose," he declared, and we set off in haste.

Down the cavern, past his underground palace, through the inside door and along the tunnel; thank heavens one was not claustrophobic. Once again, he had done a marvellous job. There were pictures all along the walls, mostly royals, ships, yachts and dogs, and a casual smattering of the imported cave art I had had imported via my European friends. The bridge over the little stream was simply delightful as was the gnome with the fishing rod. Simpson! Mrs. Simpson! Brazen hussy! His one faux pas; what was *she* doing here, on display? But one had no time to question. There was a job of work to be done.

We emerged out through the gentlemen's 'out-of-order' toilet and naturally I had to wait until the Earl gave the all clear. Together we rushed out, just in time to see Philip hotfoot it out under Admiralty Arch. From there we all waited for the 139. I distinctly remember my husband looked directly at us while we stood waiting, but fortunately, we were far enough away. In any case, the Earl's quick reactions ensured we remained undetected. He leaped in front of me, back to Philip, embraced and kissed me passionately. Naturally I acted along, following the Earl's lead. Not more than a minute or two had passed... perhaps three, when I peeked over my accomplice's shoulder. Philip had looked away, presumably in a state of embarrassment: weirdly dressed strangers behaving obnoxiously... and in public! As I wiped my lips and straightened my blouse, the bus pulled in. One could not help but take pride in my husband's reaction. As for the Earl, he smiled a smug triumphant grin so I kicked him hard on the shin and glared at him through my dark glasses.

We alighted in Oxford Street, quite close to Poland Street. Had to stay well back while we stalked my husband; rather like a fox hunt, you know, but on foot, of course... and no fox. One felt deeply uncomfortable, not only for betraying one's husband this way but also for being in such close proximity to one's subjects with only a frisky, bushy-bearded city gent for security. My public galloped by completely ignoring me. Once or twice I gave a little, innocuous, wave but there was no cheery smile to be had from any of them.

We walked up Oxford Street while Philip hurried along as if late for an appointment. He ducked into Woolworths, but rather than follow him in, we waited at the corner for him to come out, deciding he would not be long. We were mistaken. It should only have taken five or ten minutes maximum to make a purchase and yet there was no sign of him.

"We must go in," the Earl stated, clearly worried, his beard bobbling up and down.

"No," I replied. "It's too risky for both of us to enter. He might remember the pair of us together from the bus stop and become suspicious. Philip is my husband and not yours, so it falls to me to pursue him."

"Are you sure Ma'am?"

"Of course I'm sure. Remember it well. Westminster Abbey, November forty-seven, eleven-thirty. Now you wait here until I return."

I could see The Earl was unhappy at my decision; understandably so. I would be on my own, marooned and destitute in a sea of abject danger amongst Woolworth shop staff and early-morning, bargain-hunting non-royals. In his demeanour, I could see he was already noting the sad circumstances of my departure for some future and solemn public enquiry, but I was adamant; one's husband must be found. I had to enter the dragon's den, alone, friendless and wretched, and venture down however many aisles it took, no matter how ghastly, no matter how horrid, for as long as the task should take, so help me God.

I perused the store slowly, as if some ordinary shopper on a restricted budget. Actually I was on the ultimate budget for I had no money at all.

Now where was he?

First, home appliances. I straightened my curlers and inspected a mop. Nice design; ultra-absorbent head with commendable two-handed grip technology. No sign. Then onwards to end-of-summer offers; wasp spray, sun cream, insect-friendly fly-swats and so on; one's husband was nowhere to be seen. But as I turned into aisle seven, confectionery, there he was, hands behind his back, sauntering along, taking it all in, not a care in the world. I picked out a bar of fudge, a small weakness of mine, fully intending to return it. Meanwhile, I observed a member of staff, sidling up to him; Rosemary, as I was subsequently informed. She said 'good morning', and so did he. The barefaced cheek of it! Saying 'good morning' to a married man. One instinctively knows a woman of her type: the husband stealing type! She smiled, he smiled and swaggered a little. One's blood boiled. What to do? I drifted quickly to the adjacent aisle where one, listening carefully, could not but overhear their conversation.

"Why don't you come over to my place for dinner, some evening... after work." Her Jamaican accent rang loud and clear.

"No, I couldn't possibly Rosemary."

"I insist Mr Dukeof. I do a lovely pork jerk. You think it over, sir."

Pork jerk! Pork jerk! Never was a man so easily seduced, and why Mr. Dukeof? Good heavens, I thought. There could only be one reason; he had an alias! One's husband, one's liege man! I dashed for the door, in a state of shock, but unfortunately, in my angst, I forgot to return the bar of fudge. As I rushed through, a familiar hand caught my arm.

"Not so fast madam, I believe you may have something you have not paid for."

I was dumbstruck and before I could regain my composure, I was being frogmarched down a narrow wooden stairs to a chilly back office. En route, a smallish gentleman with a snide, evil grin, congratulated Philip. One's world was caving in. Tears began to flow. Big ones; big embarrassed, humiliated tears.

"First today Mr. Dukeof, well done!"

"Yes, sir. Thank you, sir."

Philip sat me down and took down a black file, carefully avoiding eye contact. As yet he was totally unaware that this 'shoplifter' was different to the rest.

40

The clock on the wall stopped; time had stood still, abandoning us

A beautiful autumn morning.

Shortly before our tour to South America, if I remember correctly. Rather chilly: a touch of frost in the air. Had to rearrange my first Tuesday to the fourth Tuesday. Hector looked a tad miffed, but agreed as I knew he would. Violet told me he was not always quite so accommodating but then again, just as Manchester United, the football club, had been prepared to accommodate that wayward George Best chap, the Woolworth Hectors of this world would also have to bend a little to oblige their star store detective, would they not?

I had fully recovered from that little incident with Mr Ace News Reporter, the Irish chap, but I was now extra vigilant with my disguise. Lucky escape, let me tell you. Didn't want another episode like that!

I decided to sit at the back of the 139 that morning, rather than at the front. Safer, one felt. Double checked all the passengers on the way to Oxford Street. Usual collection. Sullen sleepy Londoners young and old; work and school. Weird couple at the bus stop, I must say; early morning passion: exhibitionists, the pair of them, kissing and smooching: disgusting, but otherwise nothing unusual.

Thought everything was back to normal as I hopped off the bus. How wrong was I!

Not many shoppers about, so I chatted to that lovely Jamaican lady, Rosemary, while I waited. Caught sight of this female shopper, out of the corner of my eye, acting suspiciously. No dress sense, I noticed; ridiculous attire, but she didn't look like a shoplifter, except maybe for the handbag; similar to Elizabeth's, as it happens, and perched at an odd angle. No shopping basket either, which increased my suspicions a little, but one can never tell. She looked at me shiftily through dark glasses, so when I saw her turn her back and pick up a large bar of peppermint fudge de crème brulee (never a big seller), I went on full alert, code red!

She disappeared for a few seconds, into the next aisle, then made straight for the door; head down, sprinting, as if her life depended on it. Classic nab! One foot out the door. Oh no you don't!

I sat her in the chair of shame, reached up to the top shelf and took down the black file. Slowly, she took off her dark glasses.

My mouth dropped open, my file spilled away silently,

and I sank to my knees… disbelieving head in disbelieving hands. Oh my God… Elizabeth! Oh my God, what have I done?

I turned away and wept; ashamed of my seedy, covert lifestyle. Elizabeth also sobbed, ashamed she had had to find out. I had deceived. She had uncovered. The room overflowed with guilt, with shame and remorse, both of us equally culpable. The clock on the wall stopped; time had stood still, abandoning us. We said nothing for a while, each of us lost in our own private purgatory. Quiet time; quiet healing time, a mini eternity. Nothing to say; soon, but not yet, as if the world had ground to a halt in sympathy, holding its breath.

We had to wait, both of us, and we did; accepting our fate, accepting our punishment, our anguish.

The shop above was strangely hushed. I gently took the chair from the far side of the desk and placed it beside hers. She offered me her handkerchief. I held out my hand, not at all sure… she took it, quietly, softly; almost like the old days, the old, guilt-free, burden-free days; happier times. The clock over the door, as if remembering its appointed duty, began to tick again, began to quietly measure our grief, painfully, one second at a time. Finally Elizabeth spoke.

"Do something, Philip," she whispered.

I drew breath.

"Wait here," I said, as if she could do otherwise. We both dried our eyes, and I put my dark glasses back on.

I found Hector standing at the end of aisle five, leaning against the record stand. He had a Rolling Stones LP in his hand which he eyed with distain.

"I'll give them a year," he announced as I approached. "Banshees: wailing, screeching banshees. I much prefer The Beatles. Can't see what… "

"I have someone I would like you to meet, Mr. Bellweather," I interrupted.

"I don't do the post-match interviews anymore," he declared with a smirk, "that's your job, now. You wanted it and now it's yours: in your contract, dear boy, if you care to look."

"Yes sir, but you may want to make an exception."

"What's gotten into you man. No exceptions, ever; you know that. Have you called the police?"

"Please sir. It's a delicate situation; not a good idea."

"Who have you down there, Mr. Dukeof, someone famous? Star struck are we? The Shah of Iran, maybe? The Archbishop of Canterbury? Perhaps The Queen, eh… is it Her Majesty, Mr. Dukeof?" And he chuckled and chuckled. But he could see I was more than a little distraught, even through my dark glasses, and having moaned and rolled his eyes several times, he relented.

"All right then. I'll go and help you out this once. There's nobody above the law you know, don't care how high and mighty they are. A thief is a thief, Mr Dukeof. A thief *is* a thief… "

41

Two sheep, no flock

Outside the store, a wintery gloom has descended, the sun hiding behind a thickening cloud. A brisk wind from the north chases leaves and litter down the street. Mr Bellweather holds the door open, apologises yet again and bows one last time, his nose almost touching his knees.

We walk aimlessly, neither saying much; losing track of time and space. Two sheep, no flock.

"Tea?"

"Maybe later. Where are we, Philip?"

"Charing Cross Road… look there's Foyles. Shall we go in? "

"Yes, let's. It's been a while since we've browsed."

On the ground floor, in the children's section, a mother and daughter are leafing through several of the large selection of books on display. They have a decision to make.

"Enid Blytons are always excellent," says Mother. "We could take two of hers or maybe something more grown up."

She picks up a Hans Christian Andersen from the next section along: *The Emperor's New Clothes*.

"This one has a moral, dear. Sometimes children are wise and adults foolish because children are not as easily mislead by pretence."

Her daughter nods.

Close by, The Queen and Prince Philip walk down the aisle; a royal procession of two; something for the two younger children, perhaps, the prince thinks. They stop and look around, expecting service. Nobody comes. Undaunted, the Royal Consort takes his wage packet from his back pocket, given him earlier by a dumb-struck Hector, and holds out a five pound note.

"Hector paid in full, you know. Only worked till you came in; nine-thirty. Shall we buy something for everyone, Elizabeth? Surprise the children. What do you think?"

Daughter observes the strangely dressed couple as they approach. In an instant, she recognises The Queen and her consort. She tugs her mother's dress.

"Oh Mum," she whispers, "it's The Queen of England with her husband, Prince… em."

Her mother, lost in concentration examining the fairy tale, checks front and back, the content, the price and finally, her purse. She reluctantly puts the book back; some other time.

"No dear, it's about an emperor. The Royal Family section is the next aisle… and don't point darling, it's rude."

The Queen and her liege man enjoy an awkward saunter back to the palace; down Charing Cross, across Trafalgar

Square and under Admiralty Arch. As they walk down The Mall, The Queen speaks.

"I'm so sorry I've had to end your career this way, darling Philip."

"How do you mean, my dear?"

"Well… we've been uncovered, both of us. You've been uncovered by that nice Mr. Bellweather."

"Good heavens no, dear. He discovered who you are; we both did, remember? My disguise remained intact. He still has no idea. Much better now. Such a weight off my shoulders, you knowing my big secret. Next month I shan't have to creep down the corridor, past your bedroom."

"No Philip; enough. I forbid it! How can you?"

"But Elizabeth, please… "

"No Philip, no. It's out of the question. Have you any…? Oh good heavens, oh goodness gracious; how incredibly careless of me. I've forgotten the Earl. Completely. I've left him behind at Woolworths."

42

Just look in my purse; not a penny

"Oh what wonderful stories you have Philip, you could write a book."

The Queen laughs and laughs.

"The gift shop Philip, and the cricket match in Green Park; good heavens; that lovely 'union man' and that ghastly reporter who almost captured you. Of all the good luck, Biggs and Lucan arriving just in the nick of time."

Princess Margaret joins in the glee.

"If only Anne and Charles knew what Father gets up to!"

"Don't you dare tell them, don't you dare," and everyone laughs again.

The Queen Mother is full of admiration.

"I always knew you had spunk, young Philip. The monarchy needs you and more like you; I've always said. One simply cannot believe you got yourself a real job… and in a shop of all places, catching criminals… like our Lilibet! The Queen: can one believe it? A common criminal!"

All four burst out laughing and the dogs run around in excitement.

The Queen Mother continues.

"If we ever lose you, Philip, I shall ensure we find someone at least as good as a replacement."

The Prince turns to Elizabeth.

"Please darling, you must change your mind. Can't you see, there are many more adventures to have and stories to tell… please."

"No Philip. You know it's much too dangerous to be trundling around on your own, even if in disguise. No darling. I love you much too much to risk something dreadful happening. You'll simply have to accept your fate and become a proper royal again."

The Queen Mother places a supportive hand on her daughter's shoulder.

"What harm if he gets lost or killed? At least he'll have died happy, won't you Philip? There are always more consorts in the sea, Elizabeth, no offence intended Philip. In fact I myself haven't quite given up hope yet."

"Nor me," adds Margaret.

"Be kind, Lilibet," her mother continues. "Let him go. Can't you see how much happier he is out and about, earning an honest crust? He should not be locked-up in a gilded cage."

"The palace is not a cage, Mother; such nonsense."

"Mother is right, Elizabeth," adds Margaret. "Your husband needs freedom, the great outdoors; challenge."

She turns to her brother-in-law.

"You do, don't you Philip? Tell her!"

"No, Margaret, I cannot agree," the prince replies. "Your sister is quite right. I simply must settle down and properly assume my appointed role as liege man and consort. No doubt my sedate lifestyle shall lead me to grow old more rapidly, not to mention fat and stodgy from lack of exercise and from all the extra food and drink I shall be compelled to consume on my duties. But the Commonwealth gaze will quite rightly fall, not upon my dishevelled appearance, but upon my glorious wife, The Queen. I shall, as unobtrusively as possible, fade from view, deeper into the background. My childbearing duties are done: four is I believe, quite sufficient for hereditary purposes, and my depression is not so severe that the daily pills won't fail to suppress the worst effects. I may need to double or more my daily whisky ration to help cope with the inner turmoil, but by Jove I shall, if necessary, like a true and loyal consort. I shall drink whatever it takes from early morning all through the day, seven days a week. Fortunately, there's never a shortage of scotch in the drinks cabinet and I shall have my own personal cabinet installed in my bedroom. We shall stock up at Balmoral every Christmas, without fail. No Margaret, Elizabeth is absolutely correct. Old, overweight, weak, drunk, depressed and decrepit I may become, but I shall shower every day, irrespective of mental and physical state and shall, without fail, shower all of my love and obedience on my darling wife, for as long as my kidneys endure. Rest assured, Elizabeth, I shall always be presentable, alert and sobered-up whenever the need occurs. As time passes, it shall be of diminishing importance, the maintaining of one's dignity in your service and in that of the Commonwealth, but I shall, in the end, have served you faithfully to the best of my faltering abilities; your faithful and loyal liege man to the end."

The Queen considers.

"Pills and whisky? Fat, depressed? No more… perhaps I am being too hasty, darling. On mature reflection, Mother and Sister may have a point. What harm if you have an outside interest, risking death and mutilation at the hands of some abject psychopath, and the extra money coming in will be very welcome in these stringent times. Yes, Philip, I believe one has changed one's mind. As Mother has pointed out, if you should come to an abrupt end, there are plenty more consorts in the sea."

"Oh thank you darling, you're the best queen a consort could possibly have; truly."

The prince, Queen Mother and Margaret all applaud and cheer in excitement and a cleaner attends one of the corgis.

"I have one stipulation."

The Queen stiffens and points a finger.

"I also want an outside job. Why should you have all the fun? Just look in my purse; not a penny. Why should you be the only royal with a bulge in your trousers?"

The Prince looks to Margaret. Margaret looks to her mother. The Queen Mother looks to the ceiling rose and then for the fly swat: there's that irksome bluebottle again!

"Well Philip. Is it a deal?"

"But darling, how can we get you a job? Mine came quite by accident."

"Then I shall join you, my dear, in Woolworths. I'm sure

Hector will have something; maybe in the office with that nice photo of me above the door. We can spend so much extra time together; quality time. Won't that be wonderful?"

"Yes dear... wonderful dear."

43

"Dogs, horses, children and one's empire"

Prince Philip looks out the window, north towards Piccadilly, hands clasped behind his back. The Queen shifts in her chair and anxiously checks her watch. In the corner, the young lady therapist continues to take notes, recording, most carefully, in longhand and occasionally updating her laptop.

"Have we time for our stint at Woolies, dear?" The Queen asks. "It's already been a long day for our young friend here, having come all this way, and so early. You're perfectly welcome to spend the night, dear, don't you agree, Philip? Anne's old room. Empty for some time now... gosh; must be over twenty years... doesn't time fly? Philip, you carry on."

"But can you remember where we were, Elizabeth? I've lost track."

"We were going down the ladder dear, on our first morning together; Woolworths; late sixty-eight."

Prince Philip looks to the sky and wags a finger.

"Ah yes, yes, of course I remember; very well as it happens. We descended the ladder on that first Tuesday morning after you had relented. I pretended to fall off in the dark; you were highly amused I seem to recall. First day away together dear, and the Earl was there to greet us at the bottom of the shaft. Very surprised to hear you clambering down after me I can tell you, but then, I think he'd arrived at the point where he simply expected the unexpected, and small wonder. Never knew what to expect, I expect, the Earl.

"The smell was terrible, and the flies; ghastly, absolutely horrid; hideous. As we strode along towards the tunnel, two of us hunched, the other not, the Earl confided a new and disturbing secret."

"The increase in noxious aroma, Your Highnesses: there's very good reason."

I would have rathered he had not spoken of such issues in the presence of The Queen, but I allowed him to carry on.

"You will remember passing over a very limp Lord Lucan, perhaps two months ago?"

"Of course I do. Owe a debt of gratitude for that man's help, albeit unintentional, and to you, of course, for taking care of him."

"Well, I'm afraid he was beyond taking care of. You see he died sir, snuffed it; never regained consciousness, so I had to store him with the others; separate section, of course; shoved him in at the back. Dreadfully sorry, sir. But he was a bad egg, brazen fellow, hanging around with that Biggs chap. I feel certain he would eventually have spent time at Her Majesty's pleasure."

The Queen is confused.

"Pleasure, did you say? Her Majesty's pleasure? Why on earth should I wish to have the pleasure of this person's company? Never even met the gentleman."

Prince Philip continues.

"Good heavens Earl, that's terrible."

"It is very unfortunate, sir, the poor man falling victim to the wanton, mindless violence of which we see so much these days..."

"No, no; not that Earl, not that; your decision! Your decision was terrible. I distinctly remember telling you to take him to the police; to secure him and then hand him over."

"But he was dead sir, extremely so; no question; blood everywhere, Your Highnesses, from his head wound, mostly. Had I called the police, it would not have been long before they had traced his movements and most likely found their way to our secret tunnel, and then possibly to your good self. What with the late lamented Lord's blood all over your clothes, and in the toilet, and the tunnel and all over the underground palace, it could have been disastrous. Doesn't bear thinking about, sir. Catastrophe!"

He had a point, one had to concede, and Her Majesty nodded demurely in agreement as we walked briskly along the tunnel. But I was not happy, no indeed, not at all happy. There was damn-near an epidemic of corpse-collecting underneath one's palace, a veritable royal catacomb. Who else did he have? The crew from the *Mary Celeste*? The lost tribes of Israel? I felt totally powerless to prevent its continued expansion! Nevertheless, I breathed deeply and curbed my irritation.

"Yes," I ventured. "Tragic indeed and one cannot be selfish at times like these. We must be gallant, brave, committed to all that is right and proper, for the sake of The Queen, for Royalty, home and abroad, and for the very future of the Commonwealth itself and its generations to come. How long do you think the smell will last?"

"I'm double-dousing daily sir, diligently drenching with disinfectant: Evening Primrose Bleach-de-Lux, the best, in my opinion, for decaying corpses in varying degrees of decomposition; deep-penetration sir, extra strength, for maximum effect."

"Ah yes, the Evening Primrose is very good but you might also consider Hawaiian Sea Anemone or Alaskan Musky Moose, premium strength. They're on special at the moment, you know. How long...?"

"The smell, sir?"

"Yes."

"Four to six, Your Highness."

"Of course... weeks?"

"Months, perhaps longer."

"Oh crikey, that long! Ghastly business..."

Hector sits impassive, slack-jawed, goggle-eyed, when for the second time in just four weeks, he has the pleasure of meeting The Queen. He mumbles something along the lines of buses not coming along as expected, before remembering his etiquette and ordering some fresh tea, a roulade and the queen cakes he'd been saving for elevenses. As yet, I had not explained why we had returned and, not surprisingly, he is more than a little awed to see his star store detective escorting a heavily disguised queen into his office. Was he in trouble with the palace? Was he to be welcomed at the palace? Why was Her Majesty here after the dreadfully unfortunate events of just a few weeks previous? He blanches somewhat, concern was written all over his anxious little face. Rosemary puts the tray down, winks at me and throws a quizzical look at the strange, bespectacled, lady on my right. She leaves the office, closing the door behind her. I immediately take off my dark glasses and crimson wig...

Having retrieved Hector from the floor, he again utters something unintelligible along the lines of, 'not one but two', though heaven only knows what he was referring to.

"Mr Bellweather," I begin once his head has cleared sufficiently and the tea has been poured, "one cannot be selfish at times like these. We must be gallant, brave, committed to all that is right and proper, for the sake of The Queen, for Royalty, home and abroad, and for the very future of the Commonwealth itself and its generations to come. Allow me to get straight to the point, sir. My wife needs a job, a part-time job. Same hours as me."

"Oh... employment?" he replies, surprised, and with a notable sigh of relief. "I see... well... so that's what this is all about then. OK, em... well, I will need to ask a few questions." He looks to his Queen. "Take your time, Your Majesty and explain why you would like an employment opportunity at Woolworths?"

The Queen considers for a moment.

"One enjoys meeting people. One likes working in a retail

environment; one lives close by and one wishes to work alongside one's husband."

"Very good, Ma'am. Do you have any hobbies?"

"Dogs, horses, children and one's empire."

"Thank you Your Majesty. Let me see what we have."

From the top drawer on his left, he pulls a file.

"Part-time, once a month… hmmm, difficult. Cleaner… Stockroom Assistant… Purchase Ledger Clerk… Confection sampling… "

Prince Philip leans forward and speaks.

"If I may, Mr Bellweather, I have a suggestion. My wife, being head of the family, is very good with the household budget and with figures generally."

The Queen interrupts.

"There are ten million people in Zambia, mostly natives, but eleven in Australia, mostly not, and the average temperature in New Zealand is broadly similar to that of Canada."

Hector raises an eyebrow and Prince Philip carries on.

"If I remember correctly from a recent conversation, you are required by head office to perform the following;

'a time and motion study, assessing the effectiveness of performance against the company-wide demographic socio-economic diversity stratification findings, thereby, aiding the interpretation of the already extrapolated data and facilitating the introduction of new non-seasonal age-adjusted variance, to offset the already-known seasonal factors inherent in previously collected data'.

"My wife would be perfect for the job not only here but across all the South London Woolworths, don't you think?"

The Queen smiles, "'My wife', I love being called 'my wife'."

Hector nods and rubs his chin.

Again, Her Majesty finds some interesting statistics.

"There are twice as many corgis as dorgis at the palace, but no cats. To date, one has appeared on five hundred and nineteen separate stamps, earning seventy five million pounds for the various Commonwealth postal services."

"Thank you Ma'am."

Hector stands up and paces.

"I see what you're saying, Mr Dukeof… I mean Your Royal Highness. You know that form is still sat on my desk somewhere. Yes, excellent idea, exceptional, but I can't pay much. Cutbacks, recession and so on. Can we agree on two pounds ten shillings per day?"

The Queen frowns.

"Retired, one would consider it, but as a reigning monarch, one requires more. Five pounds a day, cash, not a penny less."

Hector again nods and sighs.

"Let's get you started, Ma'am," he responds. "No time like the present."

And above his head the office clock ticks steadily by…

He lit up like a blushing beetroot on a sunburnt summer's day

The very next morning I had the most amazing surprise.

A letter arrived from none other than, the supposedly deceased, Lord Lucan.

Dear Prince Philip,

Please accept my sincere apologies for not writing sooner, but I have had a great deal on my mind.

My principal reason for writing, Your Highness, is to thank you for looking after me following Mr Biggs' assault. It must have taken a great deal of effort to drag my unconscious body all the way down the tunnel to my snug resting place, all-be-it, a very dark and very musty resting place, with a strange and slightly revolting odour. I presume I was knocked out since I cannot remember a thing after the first blow. As I

238

say, thank you for finding a safe and secure resting place until I was recovered sufficiently to leave, and I fully understand why you could not wait on my regaining consciousness. You will be pleased to learn that when I awoke, alone in the dark, I stumbled upon the underground living quarters, presumably for security, and your ingenious hidden tunnel. I hope you don't mind sir, but I took the liberty of investigating my surroundings before I left. What a surprise to find I was actually underneath Buckingham Palace, which is when I realised it must have been your good self I had encountered at the St James's Park convenience.

I would like to assure you sir, that I have learned my lesson. That Biggs chap is not one I should have become involved with but, I needed him to get me out of a rather tricky spot, so to speak, and I shall say no more on that particular subject.

I've taken the liberty of helping myself to the spare key in the box by the tunnel door entrance, as I assume you and your security will have several spares. Rest assured, sir, your secret is safe with me. I feel certain that it is most unlikely I will ever need to avail of your underground facilities again… but one never knows!

Once again, thank you for rescuing me,

    Yours Truly,

        Lucan

I instantly called for a meeting with the Earl.

"Well I never," he said.

"So if he was not as dead as you thought," I replied, "who have you been diligently double-dousing daily for the past two months?"

The Earl became incredibly sheepish. I'd never seen him redden like this before, but he lit up like a blushing beetroot on a sunburnt summer's day.

"Ah," he responded, "I'm most dreadfully sorry sir, but it seems I have one final cadaver to declare."

"Go on," I said.

"Solves a mystery, as it happens," he responded. "I had wondered what I'd done with dear old Willis. Knew I'd left him somewhere."

"Willis?"

"Yes sir, he was the last to succumb, in sixty-five. He keeled over suddenly, on a Wednesday afternoon. Lost him in the dark the following day... slightly too much to drink, sir, no excuse really."

There was an awkward silence.

"But I am pleased he's 'turned up' sir," he said. "It's not good losing one's corpses, a tad careless of me."

Lost his marbles, that's what; nuttier than a barrow-load of squirrels in November, but what could I do?

On the plus side, I found myself agreeing with Lord Lucan's deductions. I felt safe in that, he'd clearly learned his lesson, a painful one, and I was sure from the tone of his letter that he was starting to turn his life around for the better.

He'll never venture this way again, I concluded. Why should he? What possible reason could he have to ever use the royal tunnel again?

45

Old Winston knew a thing or two

The Queen rises slowly from her chair and joins her husband at the window. Together they look out across horizon, and into the evening sky.

"I believe we've just about completed today's session Philip. How many years did we work together at Woolies?"

"Almost ten, in the end dear, until technology made us obsolete."

"And Hector, of course. Don't forget Hector. Not a word, you know; utterly loyal, unlike some! I do hope he found a suitable role after all that upset in seventy-eight or was it seventy-nine?"

"We all have to move on dear, the great and the good… inevitable… marvellous times, though."

"The best…"

"Not all sad reminiscences, Elizabeth. MI5 still allow us

to dress up and use the tunnel on occasion and to wander, closely observed of course, amongst our public. Not far these days, it must be said: Trafalgar to feed the pigeons, St James's to feed the ducks and Horseguards to tease the sentries. Nice of the Earl to accompany us on occasion when he can tear himself away from his cable tv, his mushroom beds and his monitoring equipment. Slower these days, though. Shame he was unable find something… more fulfilling, for himself and family before it all became too late."

"He's happy, in his own way. Could have followed Jones up to Scotland, if he'd wanted. Had the choice, did he not? We gave him the choice."

The Queen picks up the latest royal photo album.

"Don't my grandchildren look lovely in this one, Philip?"

The Prince nods.

"What have you on for tomorrow, dear? I'm getting ready for Sandringham and of course, there's the garden party to organise. What time is the PM due? It is Wednesday today? Time flies by so quickly."

"Well you know what my routine is, Elizabeth; have to do it or I shall start to see those blasted mountains again. Indulge, I'm told; satisfy one's need for adventure, the hunter's instinct. Catch some criminals! I'm under instruction Elizabeth, as you know."

Her Majesty sighs.

"I do worry about you Philip. What if you're recognised? Wandering down Oxford Street, alone; it's dangerous. It's not the same as dressing up for The Queen's Gallery, you know. You might so easily come undone; then what would I do? And make sure you charge your mobile."

242

"I was made for taking risks, Elizabeth. Is that not why you married me, all those years ago?

The prince takes out his pipe and whooshes away an annoying bluebottle. He raps the pipe hard on the leg of his chair and fills it with ready-rubbed tobacco. He lights-up, creating a plume of contented, swirling smoke.

"You know, Elizabeth, when they come to write our story, none of this will appear, not a single word of it. It never happened. We've kept it from them, all of it; out of the papers, away from the media, you and I both. He who wins the war darling, writes the history. Old Winston knew a thing or two."

In the corner, the therapist puts her pens away and closes her laptop, while above Prince Philip's head, a gentle autumn breeze wafts the smoke away.

46

All this and so much more

Towards the bottom of Charing Cross Road, on the first floor of a large, well established bookshop, daughter, using the wheelchair access, heaves and hauls, pulls and pushes her mother to the 'New Issues' section.

"It's here somewhere, Mum. I saw it on that book review programme."

Mother looks at daughter, a bored, exasperated look on her face.

"You've dragged me all this way just to show me a book? Won't it be available on the Kindle?"

Daughter returns a raised eyebrow and exaggerated sigh.

"It's not just any old book, as you well know. It proves I was right all those years ago, right here in this very bookshop... Ah, here it is."

She takes down a paperback and fans it with her thumb. She checks the title and begins to read the back cover.

"See; told you so Mum, but you didn't believe me."

"For heaven sake, child, it was forty years ago... maybe more."

"Yes, I know," replies daughter, "but look; here it is; proof I was right all along."

She reads aloud from the back cover.

A STORY LIKE NO OTHER.
THE ROYAL FAMILY IN TURMOIL.

Prince Philip, the consort, depressed, shackled by obligation, finds a secret tunnel and escapes.
Will it save his sanity? What of The Queen? Can their marriage survive?
Is there... another woman?

His plight, her angst.
Hidden bodies.
Disinfectant.
Knotweed.

The world must never know!

Wonder at the heart-stopping adventures as Prince Philip secures gainful employment at Woolworths. Marvel at Her Majesty's resolve in supporting her desperately unhappy husband whilst never flinching in her devotion to Crown and duty to the Commonwealth.

All this and so much more.

A must for royal observers and behavioural psychologists alike.

"You see Mother, right here in this very shop, The Queen and Prince Philip. Forty years ago. I saw them myself; disguised, going through their… turmoil."

Mother picks up the book and adjusts her glasses.

"Who wrote this rubbish", she snarls as she reads from the author's notes.

"Ha, and I suppose you also believe this book has been inspired by… good lord… genetically modified insects living beneath the palace; let me see… a common housefly called Oscar, and a 'blueblood bluebottle' by the name of 'Lord Henry the Purpleheart'. Really dear, come on! You can't possibly be serious?"

And points while lost in deep repose, the path to our eternity

"Oscar. You're a fly"

"I know, Jerome, I know I'm a fly; what's your point?"

"Flies don't write, pal, flies do 'fly things', like… buzzing around and stuff like that."

"Did I ask to be a fly, did I? Listen to me Jerome, listen, I'm serious, man. I want to write. I know I can do it."

"Oscar, Oscar, Oscar; haven't you heard a word I've said? You're a fly, a fly! Don't you get it?"

Oscar sulks and Jerome puts a caring wing round his little brother's shoulder.

"I know what you're going through, mate; honest. I feel your pain; you're a fly in a million, one in a swarm, but there's some things even you can't do. Write, whatever that is, is not a fly thing. We flies do not do 'write'. OK?"

"Don't patronise me, bug-brain. How do you know what I can do?"

"No look, no… I don't mean to…" Jerome continues. "You can do stuff; course you can; really good stuff. I've seen you do it; like hanging from the ceiling by just one leg and scratching your thorax with the tip of your nose. Chasing spiders! Ain't many flies do that! Bluebottles, beetles, daddy long legs; they can't do nothing; just eat and poop; hot air and vomit, the lot of them. But you… you're something different, something, ya know, special, ever since you were a just a teeny weeny little maggot; always wanting to push it; getting into places no self-respecting fly should ever go. Mum's heart was broke, and that's the truth. But you got that vision thing, the anger, the fight. Can't exactly put my proboscis on it, but, yeah, you got that something extra. Gonna make it big, you are; something important. That's why I hang out with you, bro, that's the reason. Just love it when we hang out, love it. Ain't no two ways about it, mate: you eat guts and you got guts."

"Thanks Jerome; appreciated. Sorry about… I'm a bit agitated."

"That's OK dude."

"But I am going to write a book," continues Oscar, "I am!"

Jerome shakes his head.

"Sure you are, mate, sure you are."

Oscar explains.

"Look over there; see that stuff in the corner? They're called newspapers, *Evening Standard*s; thousands of them, stacked up by the underground human: the Earl. The squiggles, not the pictures; that's writing. That's what I want to do. I want to write. It's what the humans do."

248

Jerome looks over and scowls. He points an accusing leg at Oscar.

"Heeeeeey, man, no, no, no. I'm so sorry sunshine but you keep forgetting. You – are – a – fly! Look at yourself! You ain't no fancy-pants writey fly thingy. You just got to accept what you are, man. Now come on … life ain't so bad down here. What you say we go chat up some of them juicy chicidy-chic fffflllliettes? Whole cloud of them down at the jelly leggy."

Oscar explodes.

"No man, no! It's you that doesn't understand. I'm serious. I'm deadly serious!"

"Calm down, brother, calm down. You'll bust a gut if you ain't careful," replies Jerome.

"Come with me, and I'll show you," demands Oscar, and they fly over to the neat row of *Standard*s by the dry wall. On the floor near the stack is a pool of brown, gloopy liquid, the result of a leaking pipe directly overhead.

"Watch this!" says Oscar.

He dips his proboscis in the pool and draws up a full straw. It's good healthy fly-food, full of vitamins and nourishment, but he resists the temptation to knock it back and instead hovers over to one of the topmost newspapers. There he finds a white space between the date, June 16th 2006, and the letters below. He starts to write.

'O S C A R'

Jerome looks on in amazement.

"Wow. What a trick. Show me, man; could use this with them fly ladies."

"It's not a trick, Jerome. I've been practising for years and years. That's why you never see me; night after night. You have to understand Jerome, I want to write, have to… smart stuff… prose, poetry, literature, just like the humans. It's in me, Jerome; have to do it… I want to be famous."

Jerome mocks him.

"I want to be faaaaamouuuuus. You so vain, man. What's gotten into you? You used to be an ordinary fly, one of us. But now, I don't know. Lighten up man! Have a good, long, hard look at yourself. You're a fly!"

Oscar props his head on his foremost legs.

"Maybe you're right brother; maybe I should, ya know, settle down, raise a brood before the leg dries up. But remember Dad, before he lost the last of his seventeen wings; said he'd been modified in a lab to be extra smart and live longer; him and that upmarket bluebottle, the fat one, remember? And then they'd escaped and came here. Well it must be that Jerome, must be in the genes, my genes. I just seem to have the knack of picking stuff up; useful stuff, important stuff, like when I follow the humans to the light up the shaft or down the tunnel. There's so much to see and hear in the human world. Books, newspapers, burger boxes; good honest rotten food to slurp and fresh if you can't find the good stuff. I know it's dangerous with the humans, but I have to do it."

Jerome gives up.

"So, tell me Oscar, have you a plan?"

"The way I see it is this. If I'm going to climb out of this underground swamp, I have to do something exceptional like write something good; you know, put proboscis to paper. I'm not interested in that shallow celebrity fifteen minutes of fame. I want the real stuff, the lasting stuff, like Andy Warhol or The Queen upstairs and her husband, that Prince… what's his name, the Greek bloke, you know, the husband. I have to write something that humans want to read. That way, I'll be accepted. All of us will."

Jerome's big eyes glaze over.

"Dad would be so proud to hear you talk all clever… and Mum."

"A book; a great book; that's what I want and in my own flytime," continues Oscar. "I want to be asked onto TV shows along with politicians and intelligent people. I want gossip magazines to ask me stuff about my personal life; like, does mankind have respect for flies? Should gay flies be allowed to adopt? Have I had Botox, are my whiskers waxed? That sort of thing. And I want the BBC to send me to a desert island with just a Shakespeare and a Koran and Channel 4 to send me to the jungle to eat bugs. Is that too much to ask?"

Jerome scratches his head with at least four legs.

"Oscar, I sure-the-hell don't know what you're talking about, but if that's what you want, then you go for it. Man, you just go for it! Fly Oscar, fly. Fly to the moon! Fly to the stars!"

The brothers slap wings and rub abdomens and dance like a pair of demented dragonflies. Finally they calm down, sit in silence for a minute or two and soak up the atmosphere. Then Jerome poses the vital question.

"But how you going to do it, bro?"

"I wish I knew Jerome, I wish I knew, but the simple fact is, I have no idea what to write; poetry maybe, or a novel; maybe a fly murder mystery… I don't know. Would anyone read a fly murder mystery? I could set it in… maybe Oxford."

"Hey, hey, hey, wait a second Oscar, just you wait a secondooo."

Jerome is buzzing and bouncing.

"I might have the perfect start for you. Yeah... you know that bluebottle you mentioned, the one who escaped with Dad. Well he's still here; kinda old now, but he's right here, in this very cavern; the real deal, you know; a genuine, real life, blueblood bluebottle. Says he can trace it all the way back to the plague. Loves to talk, when he's not eating. Never stops going-on about it; genetic this, engineering that. He's got the works though: extra long legs, modified wings, all souped-up; same as Dad. I'm sure he'll help with that writing thing you want to do; he'll want to help, if only, ya know, to pay respects."

"You think so?"

"Sure he will. Come on. I know exactly where he'll be."

They fly over to the human body by the wall, the most recently added to the collection by the Earl. Not much of it left. There's an exhausted torso at one end and close by, a large, shiny ivory skull with bits of knotted hair and an ever-present smile on teeth that don't need cleaning. There's matted eyebrows perched high on a scalpless brow, wearing a look of permanent surprise as if questioning where it all went wrong. A large bluebottle, settling in to yet another wholesome feast, has delved deep into a receding eye socket, having pushed and shoved his way past numerous smaller, less-able insects.

"Hey Henry! Come out. Want you to meet my brother, Oscar."

"I'm indisposed, dear boy," an echoing voice replies, "rather busy with a juicy piece of cerebellum. There's not much left."

"Henry!"

"What?"

"Come on out your royal flyness. You've got to meet my brother… he can write."

The overweight bluebottle covered in slime lumbers up and over the left eye socket. Crawling past the hollow, once occupied by a fine, fleshy nose, he stops to lick his greasy legs and wipe and moisten his elegant blueblood whiskers. He then spits a lump of grizzle and raises a puzzled antenna before belching loudly and clearing his throat.

"He can write? Your brother writes? Why didn't you say so, my dear chap."

He sidles up to Oscar, preening as he goes, and extends a foreleg.

"Lord Henry the Purpleheart at your service."

All three fly over to the dangling hand. They sit out on a bony outstretched finger and hang their hairy legs over the edge.

"Show him Oscar, show him what you can do," and Jerome points to an unsullied fingernail.

"Are you kidding? I'm not wasting my time proving what I can do to this… this outsized bluebottle."

"Oh but you must, dear friend. I knew your father years ago; the resemblance is uncanny; same thorax, same iridescent eyes, same appalling manners. And I have an exquisite story for one with superior writing skills; the untold tale of a disenchanted royal consort waits to explode upon the world. I was there, from the beginning; met The Queen Mother on several occasions… never officially. But I shall only reveal to one who is worthy to hear and sufficiently skilled to record my epic tale. Now write, good sir, write."

Oscar considers. This bluebottle, he decides, has an ego the size of his abdomen but he also seems to have something I can use. I need a story the humans will want to read; to muse upon and discuss and I already know something of the royal family, from my own excursions both upstairs and down the tunnel. So yes, he could be very useful indeed. In any case, what difference? If he's all 'hot air and vomit' as Jerome so eloquently puts it, I can simply retract, drop him. He needs me more than I need him.

"All right, I'll do it."

Oscar looks across to the end of the human hand.

An unblemished fingernail, on a rigor-mortised skeletal finger, points into the dark, eternal abyss as if offering some desperate, post-life advice. He climbs out, along with Lord Henry, to the edge. He checks he has enough gloop, and starts to write.

This pallid fingernail supports
The weight of you, the weight of me
And points while lost in deep repose
The path to our eternity

"Amazing and amusing my good fellow; truly astounding. Allow me to finish my supper; then we shall make plans."

Oscar recoils, his proboscis slightly out of joint.

"Hey, hey, hey big fellow; not so fast. I'm a busy fly; things to do. If you've got what I need, I want to hear it now."

"But how do I know you're trustworthy?"

"You don't."

"But I need time to think, dear boy."

"It's now or never, Lord Henry. I'm genetic like you but we're both on a limited lifespan, and, I notice you're nearly out of human brain."

Lord Henry the Purpleheart thinks it over… briefly.

"You know your dad and I escaped the lab together; he had all the wings and I had all the legs." He dangles his remaining fifteen to prove the point. "Let's go somewhere quiet, dear boy. Replenish your quill for I have a story to tell… "

Dear reader...

Thank you from the bottom of my pocket for buying my book and complements on your inspired choice of reading material.

If you have enjoyed it, spread the good news. Don't be shy. Your friends need to know! They will, of course, want their own copy - £8.99 at all good book stores or possibly less if purchased direct from the excellent Troubador. (www.troubador.co.uk)

In the unlikely event you did not enjoy my book, don't struggle with your conscience, wondering if you should remain silent. Tell your friends to buy it so they too can indulge in the mind-numbing awfulness of it. Why suffer alone? It's what your true and loyal friends would want: sharing the pain, the hurt, the misery... and all at a very reasonable price!

Finally, no royals or animals of any description were harmed in the writing of this book, but if you have any concerns please address them to the author at: thomasjomara@yahoo.co.uk

Thanks again,